# Streets Jackson

# STREETS JACKSON

Pat - We share many great memories - Dick Pumphrey

A NOVEL BY:

RICHARD G. PUMPHREY

EGGMAN PUBLISHING
NASHVILLE, TENNESSEE

EGGMAN PUBLISHING



Library of Congress Catalog Card Number
96-085982

ISBN: 1-886371-52-0

*Printed in the United States of America*

*To God because I owe him everything.*

*To my wife Dotti and my daughter Lynn, for their constant support and encouragement.*

*To the hundreds of athletes I coached who worked so hard for me. Some were champions and won the medals. They were all champions to me. I always appreciated the effort.*

*To the many coaches who touched my life and whose lives certainly touched mine.*

# ACKNOWLEDGEMENTS

I appreciate the efforts of the following people who have helped me with my manuscript:

Marty Rains, ex-English teacher and writing teacher who helped me see my ten thousand errors and critiqued the book.

Bob Rains, retired coach and county superintendent.

Coach Rick Rice, head football coach, Waynesboro, Tennessee High School.

They all read the book, were very helpful with their suggestions, and very kind in their analysis.

# Contents

CONTENTS

CONTENTS

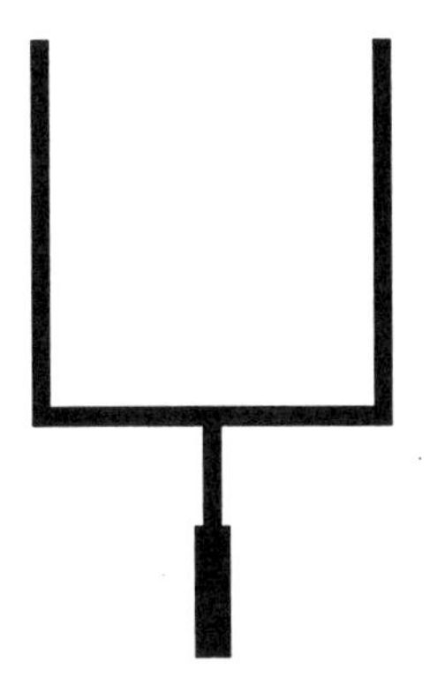

# INTRODUCTION

THE GRAYING HULK OF A MAN SPRAWLED ASLEEP in his lounge chair, his feet in the water of a Florida lake. He looked like what he was, a veteran football coach, muscled and tough, his slightly bent nose canted toward the setting sun, pulled in that direction as if it were a plant. The years had been kind to him and the power was still there.

His antiquated Shakespeare fishing reel and rod lay on the sparse grass of the lakeshore beside him, the line wrapped around his big toe with a red and white float bobbing twenty feet from the shore. His toe was moving up and down with each bob of the float as a small shellcracker worried the bait on the hook. The pull on the line must not have been too much because he was oblivious to it all, a gladiator resting from the wars. A fierce looking nonpoisonous Florida banded water snake swam away from his wriggling toe, having inspected the curious thing, deciding there was more than he wanted to swallow. It wasn't on his regular menu. Coach Angus Warren's red-blond hair was half gray, each hair a chevron stripe caused by flunking athletes and missed extra points. His mouth was open and the tropical sun toasted his tonsils, landing lightly against his bronze skin, his head falling slightly to the right with the pull of gravity.

Angus Warren had earned his rest and rested easily. His wife brought a cup of coffee to him, giggled at his grotesque posture, then returned to the house, the cup still in her hand. The coach was in another world. Maybe you could call it a dream because he obviously was not awake. His mind was back many years before, going over the events that led to the final game of a turbulent year, his attempt to win the state football championship.

He saw himself in Tennessee, a nineteen year old sophomore at Tennessee A & M. A smile of satisfaction flitted across his face as he remembered the fateful meeting with a beautiful coed, then the expression changed as his thoughts moved to the years of coaching in Tennessee and the move to Florida. If his wife had stayed beside him, she would have seen the different expressions as the dream clouded his face when he remembered the torturing experience with the best athlete he ever coached, Streets Jackson, and the nerve-wracking drive toward that final game. As the sun plowed its eternal furrow toward the horizon, a pair of ospreys flew circles over the lake, looking for careless fish, and the coots squawked in the nearby cattails.

# 1

# Angus and Blackie

I GUESS I WAS LIKE MOST OF THE OTHER GUYS around the college campus; we were what so many of the girls came to college for, to find an eligible male. I had advantages over some of the others, because at six foot two and two fifteen, I knew the ladies looked up to me in more ways than one. My snub nose is slightly bent, my teeth are straight and white because I take care of them. I guess I learned early that the girls like me and I've always been glad they do. I know my bent nose makes me look tough and I'm glad of that because it made the football coach like me too. Somehow it doesn't make me ugly, and in freshman English, I overheard a girl whisper to another one, "He makes me shiver." It sounded crazy to me because I know what I'm like inside and that sure wouldn't make anyone shiver. My brownish-blond hair is curly, long enough to be accepted on the campus, short enough so it pleases my dad back home.

I was the first one in my family to go to college, on a football scholarship to Tennessee A & M University in the hazy blue mountains. I received room, board, tuition, books, and laundry in exchange for four years of blood, sweat and endless hours of football. The A & M coaches didn't have to worry about me smoking or drinking or having nerve-wracking affairs with starry-eyed girls. It just wasn't my way. I got banged around a lot since bruises, sprained ankles and worse were part of the game, but I did get an increasing knowledge of football. They let me play some as a freshman, and I started as a defensive halfback, but I could analyze plays better than some of the others, and since I loved to tackle, they moved me to line-backer and I never played any other position.

During my freshman year, when I wasn't at football practice or in the weight room, I was at the training table or at a little nook in the library. I never was interested in card games, so the poker games in the dorm didn't appeal to me. It only took me the first week at school to find that I couldn't study in my room. There were too many athletes who didn't want to study or didn't know how, and since they wouldn't leave me alone, I hunted a spot among the book stacks in the agriculture college library, and that became my second home. I majored in English. I know that sounds funny to some of the eggheads who see all jocks as if they were somewhere between moron and dull normal. I like to read, I can't help it. I'd read matchbook covers for entertainment if there were nothing else available.

I was an enigma (I learned that word in first year English) to the defensive coach. He had so many players who were indifferent students, and he was more concerned with the veteran players than with the freshmen. When the first grades were posted, two of the carousing regular players were flunking and since I was carrying a B average, the coach said to me, "Boy, I don't understand you. You don't drink or smoke, do you?"

"No sir." I didn't know where this was leading.

"And you've got a B average, and you're an English major?"

"Yes, sir."

With two of his best players probably lost to the team, the coach was pleased with me, but I could see he wished that the juniors and seniors that worried him had good habits and good grades. On the field where the hamstring pulls and the blood and mud were, I hadn't proved myself and the others had. That day, the coach walked from me, shaking his head.

I met the girl who was to be my wife during the second week of my sophomore year. With an hour between classes, I sat in one of the expansive and expensive air-conditioned reading rooms of the library, poring over a chapter of English Literature. I saw a tall, dark-haired girl with scintillating eyes watching me. When I looked up a second time and she still had her eyes on me, I winked at her. An unplanned smile lit her lovely face for an instant, then she blushed and put her nose back in the book she was studying. When the buzzer announced the change of classes, I watched the girl make her way to the entrance. I caught her and, uncharacteristically for me, I said, "Hi there. Are you new on campus?"

"Hi, and no, I'm not new here. I'm a sophomore, the same as you."

I couldn't deny it, she took my breath away. I said to her, "How'd you know I'm a sophomore? I don't remember seeing you before."

"Well, Mr. Angus Warren, I don't think you see anything here except the football field and the library."

"Looking again at her glistening black hair, her perfect complexion, and those deep, deep brown eyes, I asked, "Do you have a name, or do I just call you Blackie? And how'd you know my name?"

It was really different for me to talk to a girl like I was doing, I didn't even know where all the words were coming from. I'm not normally tongue-tied around girls, but I knew I sounded more like one of the campus romeos than I did like me. This was a good looking, uncomplicated young woman, and believe me, she was all woman. All the essentials were right out there in the open. "I know we both stood there, grinning like we'd just found an Easter egg.

She laughed a rather deep, pleasant, throaty laugh. "I have a somewhat involved name. I'm Linda Grayson Wentworth, but you can call me whatever you like, just so you call me. I've been waiting a whole year to meet you, and I don't want you to disappear into the book stacks again. It's no wonder you don't know me. I don't think you know anybody but the coaches, the librarians, and maybe the priest."

I was really enjoying the conversation. Who wouldn't? When a beautiful girl tells you she's been wanting to meet you, it curls your toes. She said, "I sit a few rows behind you every Sunday. I've always run out of the church before you because I've been afraid to meet you."

I laughed at her directness, and held out my left hand to Miss Gorgeous, to this stunning, delightfully frank girl, and she caught my hand in hers. A thrilling surge like electricity ran through me, and I hoped it did through her.

When Linda Grayson Wentworth smiled, she lit up the world around her, and she smiled when I said to her,

"I've got to go to English Lit, and I know you must have a class, but I'll meet you right here in this spot at seven this evening, if that's okay. I think we have some unfinished business.

"I'd love that," she said, "You won't forget, will you?" There was no way in the world I'd forget.

I discovered the principle of anti-gravity that day. I floated to class about two feet off the ground. Whatever the professor lectured on, I had to read later, because I never heard a word he said.

Our courtship was never tempestuous, and we never dated anyone else. Blackie's well-to-do parents were not too thrilled with me, but they never found any bad faults in me except that I was a jock and any money I had was well hidden. They didn't like my ambition to be a football coach, but they thought by my senior year the romance would dissolve. My middle class parents loved Blackie, just like I did.

I took all the coaching classes I could. I studied the football books by the experts, and when off the field during ball games, I tried to analyze what was happening. When I graduated, I was invited by the head coach to stay on as a student assistant, working with the linebackers and getting my master's degree.

We were married one week after graduation, lived in a quaint old house which the University owned, and I learned more about coaching. In fact, I learned a lot of things that year. Blackie dedicated herself to me, and learned to cook. We used one of her sets of biscuits for door stops, but I'd have eaten the limbs out of the yard if she prepared them for me. It was a year long honeymoon, the finest year of our lives.

I knew I wanted to coach football, preferably on the college level, but I knew I'd have to pay my dues on the high school level, learning how to run a good program, and learning what kind of offense and defense I could run best.

# 2

# CITRUS CITY

COACH SPEEDY JOHNS LOOKED ACROSS THE top of Florida's Citrus City High School stadium to the huge lake beyond. The school had quite a layout. It was low slung with many separate buildings, made possible by little need for heat and plentiful land donated when lake front property was not so precious. Like a fortress, the football stadium stood against the sky on the south part of the campus. The words, "Home of the Spartans" were emblazoned on each end of the stadium.

"What a setup!" The slightly rotund Johns looked at me for agreement. We had come to Citrus City to interview for coaching jobs, me as the head football coach and athletic director, Speedy as the head track coach and backfield coach. An energy-sapping, sweat-producing tropical sun radiated its June heat on us.

I echoed Speedy's thoughts, "It's better than they described on the phone. I feel like a girl trying to get into a sorority at rush time. If they want me they can have me."

Both of us were in our early thirties, and we'd been together since college days when we played football and roomed together at A & M. Speedy had left college a year ahead of me, and gone to coach at Middleton in Tennessee. I knew Speedy's good qualities, and when he influenced my hiring at that school, I was glad for the chance to coach with him. We had built a solid athletic program and were good for the athletes. From the first, our teams were always competitive, but because Middleton was one of the smallest schools in our classification, it was hard to build a champion.

While we were still in Middleton, our four-man coaching staff and our wives were having one of our frequent barbecue cookouts and I called Speedy over for a private talk. "Come over here Speedo. I want to influence you a little."

Coach Johns had been the conference 100 yard dash champion in college, and was a superb running back. He moved with athletic grace away from the other coaches. I had some news that I thought he'd like. "Coach, we've gone about as far as we can go in this town, what do you say we look for greener pastures?"

Speedy took a sip from a sweating cold drink. "That's exactly what I've been thinkin', Angus. We've given this school a hundred percent for seven years, and we know a lot more than we did when we started. We need to find a school with more material, one that has a better chance to win in its own division." Speedy scratched his fanny, a mannerism which always bothered me, but no amount of kidding had made him change, so I'd given up on it.

"Speedo, I know of a school in the citrus area of Florida that's in the market for a new staff. They have eighteen hundred in the student body, and from what I hear, the stadium will seat twelve thousand, and there's a Grasstex track as good as the one at A & M. How does that sound to you?"

"My gosh, Angus, it sounds too good to be true, and probably is. What's the ratio of black and white kids down there?"

"It's about half and half, and there hasn't been any great racial problem."

Speedy was always enthusiastic and his voice raised about two notes higher than normal when he said, "Boy, could I make a track team out of that bunch, and it couldn't help but spill over into the football program."

Now that we were at the school that we were so ambitious to work for, I stood there with the sun beating down on my busted nose that I always said I was going to get fixed, studying the Florida layout. Like Speedy said, it seemed too good to be true.

Speedy and I moved from Tennessee to Citrus City High School, and we had been there three years, starting on the fourth. The first two years had been miserable because the departing coaches had done a poor job, and the number of athletes in the classes we inherited was at a low point in the cycle. When you see a team which is a champion, they've been trained right and taught right, and there usually are a large number of junior and senior athletes who are in their physical prime for their age. The rule on age in most states is that a boy is eligible if he's under nineteen or if his nineteenth birthday doesn't come until after the first of

September. If you can just be lucky enough to have several talented football players who become nineteen shortly after school starts, you've got men, not boys. That's the position we were in.

The first year, we had two wins and eight losses. The second year we saw five and five, and we had to listen to a lot of grumbling from the Saturday morning quarterbacks. Still, the whole coaching staff took a vital interest in the middle school and jayvee programs, and the jayvees had been undefeated both years. There was light at the end of the tunnel. Speedy's track program had produced some state class sprinters who also played football.

The third year we won ten games, tied one, and lost two, including the state semi-finals. Now we were seasoned, fast, big, mature, and ready. We had three preseason all-staters—the German immigrant, Horst Michler, two hundred forty pounds, who was brilliant, ruthless, unsmiling—a true Aryan; Hunky King, a dynamic line-backer; and the rugged state hundred meter dash champion, Streets Jackson.

# 3

# Hunky King

HUNKERSON HENDERSON KING III STRETCHED his chunky, muscular body in the old wicker rocking chair on the open front porch. It was nine thirty on Saturday morning, two weeks before football practice was to start. As he flexed and extended his arms and pushed his legs out in front, the muscles bulged, the dark skin a striking contrast to his white shorts and tee shirt.

Hunky King was black and there was no doubting his genes. Black and proud, with a reason to be proud. He was named Hunkerson because his straight talking father thought it sounded good with Henderson, and he had the III tacked on the end because that sounded good too. The name had served him well in school, people thought a lot of Hunky King. He was five-foot-eight and one hundred ninety pounds of explosive power, could bench press forty pounds more than any other teammate his size, and could run the hundred meters in ten-nine, one of four players on the super fast Citrus City team under eleven flat. The previous track season, he had thrown the twelve pound shot sixty-two feet, good for second place at the state meet. Hunky was a horse: a vibrant, powerful, dynamic stallion.

Hunky King was a serious student. If you sat by him in class, you didn't cut up. He didn't normally fuss at you, you just didn't jive around near him in class.

On this muggy, tropical August morning, Hunky wasn't mad at anybody. He knew he was going to college on a football scholarship because he was good. He didn't particularly like white people, but he didn't waste his time and energy hating them either. There were a lot of white people who were his good friends. Though many other black kids couldn't see it, things were going right for anyone who was prepared and ambitious. He knew he wasn't going to have a yard full of children like so many people had. He could see that having more children than you could afford was a sure way to poverty. Observing the neighborhood, Hunkerson Henderson King III had created an axiom which he said aloud to himself: "The extent of your poverty is directly proportional to the number of your children."

As Hunky lazed in his rocking chair, drinking a cup of his mother's wonderful coffee, he bantered with the children in the neighborhood. Between two houses, across the macadam street, he caught sight of a girl hanging out a cheerleading uniform on a clothesline. "Mmmm, Latisha Washington, I wish we had time for each other."

Hunky's mind, like that of everyone on the football team, constantly turned to the coming season and to the coaching staff. He knew the success of the team depended not only on the talent of the players but on the coaching staff, especially on the head coach, Angus Warren. A coach could make or break a team, and Hunky wondered if Coach Warren had any new strategies, any plans he hadn't yet told the team.

# 4

# Latisha Washington

My opinion of cheerleading, which I expressed only to Blackie, would have curled the peroxide blond hair of the cheerleader's coach. I told Blackie, "They don't really lead cheers, it's just a dance team. The choreography is pretty good, but the leading of the student body is for the birds. Most of the students couldn't care less about screaming wicky wacky woo or whatever it is they holler. I tell you, school spirit is having a winning team. When we went two and eight, the crowd sat on their hands, but last year when we went to the state semi-finals, people woke up vocal cords that hadn't been used since eighteen eighty-eight. That's school spirit! I thank the Father above I don't have to be in charge of the cheerleaders because we'd only have one practice at which time I'd disband them so they could get on with their studies."

My wife laughed at me. "Let me give you some advice, my love. Keep that opinion to yourself or you'll have a revolution that will make the Vietnam War look like a boy scout meeting."

I knew cheerleading was a vibrant, emotional part of the life of Citrus City High School. They had to be chosen by an impartial panel from a list of seventy-five hopeful girls. The process was repeated thousands of times, all over the country, with exactly the same type of nervous, cute, athletic girls. To be named a varsity cheerleader seemed more important to some than to win the Nobel Prize.

Forty-three of the seventy-five candidates had already tried out. Although it was scorching hot outside, the spacious gym where the tryouts were proceeding was bearable. Doors at both ends of the gym were open, as were the windows under the eaves. The already exhausted judges were studiously taking notes, writing them on clipboards as each girl went through the gyrations that accompanied each cheer. The red and white colors flashed everywhere, voluntarily worn by most of the candidates since they could not try out in school uniforms.

The Citizens Bank always furnished one of their officers as a judge. This time it was Harland Roberts with his standard banker's smile, dressed impeccably in gray slacks, a gray tie which he had loosened from his conservative shirt, his blue blazer on the seat beside him. The cheerleader's coach, buxom Debbie Richards, thought to herself as she looked at Harland, "I'll bet they run those guys off a copy machine at the bank, and I sure wish they'd run me one."

Two of the nearby schools' cheerleading coaches were serving as judges in exchange for the same favor at their schools. The owner of a dress shop, a former cheerleader at Citrus City High, pored over her notes. Next to her, the women's athletic director at nearby Florida Lakes Community College talked to Coach Richards. The selection had to be done carefully, fairly, and secretly. There could be no slip-ups; too many emotions were involved.

Two of the candidates sat together on the top row of the bleachers, behind and to the left of the judges. Some would have thought they were an unlikely pair, both veterans of the cheerleading process through middle school and jayvee years. From vastly different backgrounds, each was sure of her worthiness to be chosen again. Edwina Edmondson exuded confidence. She was a senior, five foot eight, one hundred twenty pounds, with the kind of figure that makes gawking men run into telephone poles. Her thick, silky red hair came to her as an added bonus. Her father, Swede Edmondson, was a wealthy grove owner and sports enthusiast who was used to having his own way. He wanted a boy, so when Edwina came along, he called her Eddie and flooded her with anything she wanted. At seventeen, she drove a new black Camaro. She was happy, vivacious, and bursting with enthusiasm.

The other half of this cheerleading twosome, Latisha Washington, was black but not very. Exuding the best qualities of both races, she was the prettiest girl at Citrus City High School. Soft-spoken and reserved, she was the product of a very careful set of parents. She was untainted but not ignorant as it was hard to be ignorant in her environment. As with most pretty girls, the boys were a bit in awe of Latisha. The other black girls tolerated her but she wasn't popular with them because she didn't try to fit in. Latisha was five-foot-six, one hundred twelve pounds. Her figure was good but not yet mature, though it showed promise of a maturity that would be a blessing. She had wavy black hair that was easy to care for, and thanked God she didn't have to go to any extreme to keep it that way. She was a fine student, an honor society member, but not a brilliant analytical thinker. She did every lesson as soon as it was assigned, and her work was impeccable. Her notebooks were so organized that people teased her about them, and she typed all notes taken in class as well as every assignment before she handed it in. She was very quiet in class. The teachers loved her, partly because teachers love students who don't make waves, partly because she was quietly, sincerely, nice.

After watching two frenzied hours of tryouts, a pattern began to emerge. There were about eighteen good candidates for the ten cheerleading positions, and Latisha turned to Eddie and said, "What do you think?"

Eddie looked thoughtful. "I'm sure glad I'm not a sophomore. I think you and I are home free, but I'd hate to be competing without experience. It's easy to eliminate the chubbies and those who can't coordinate, but there are a lot of good girls trying out. I've about had it for this afternoon, and they won't announce the results until tomorrow. Let's go down to the Triple Burger and get a shake.

Football players Streets Jackson and Hunky King were at the football practice field, passing the football and punting to each other. Good in all areas of the game, they lofted easy, long passes to each other. Their booming punts were carrying forty to sixty yards. Seeing the two cheerleaders emerge from the gym, Streets' unsmiling face took on a grim look. "There goes miss rich bitch in her Camaro and she's got the African Queen with her." Hunky was noncommittal. He liked to practice with Streets because he was a fine football player, but he had learned a long time back not to encourage the vituperation and foul language.

# 5

# STREETS JACKSON

STREETS JACKSON WAS A HUNK IN NAME AND deed. Six foot one, and one eighty-five, his ancestors were Masai warriors and he wasn't much different from them. If he had lived in Africa, he would have killed his required lion with a spear at the earliest age possible. He was fearless to the point of absurdity and his carriage was straight as a geometric line, his body hard as a pine tree stump. Streets would be nineteen on September second, just inside the limit for high school eligibility, and he was the best running back in the state of Florida.

Streets was a handsome, slashing, Achilles-heeled, bruising running back. He often did not try to be a broken field runner, weaving in and out, looking for holes. Broken bones maybe, but not broken field. When he bloodied someone's nose or twisted an opponents knee, he reveled in it. As far as Streets was concerned, football was like boxing, the more you hurt your opponent, the more significant the victory. He was one of the few players on the team that played on both offense and defense, and the defensive coach moved him around to meet the strength of the opponents offense.

He hated whitey. As he saw it, the pampered white bastards drove around in their Lexuses and Cadillacs, drinking milkshakes and playing Pac-man. On Saturdays, when Streets was picking ten bins of oranges off a twenty-foot ladder, he visualized the soft white boys driving their spoiled girlfriends to Daytona Beach or Clearwater for a day at the beach. The fact that some of the white boys worked just as hard as he and lived no better, never crossed his mind. Life for Streets was hard and lean, just as he was. He mused to himself, "Our day is almost here, Honky. Our day is almost here."

He cut a wide swath wherever he went, and the neighborhood didn't like him. Wherever he swaggered, most of them got out of the way. He carried a six inch New Orleans switchblade and said he would use it. He had enough smarts to keep his mouth shut at school because it was grounds for expulsion. Officious principal Oscar O. Seidthorn knew Streets carried the knife, but he wasn't about to make a case of it. Streets was a bully, and took savage pleasure in it.

He was naturally very fast and the track program of Coach Speedy Johns had made him faster. He loved track because it was individual and nobody else got credit for what he did. Most other athletes hated to run wide open for long periods of time, but Streets loved the pain of it. He didn't mind the two hundred meter interval runs, and would sometimes do ten of them at a practice. His body was tuned like a race car ready for the Daytona 500.

One of Streets' favorite ploys was to miss track practice when he wanted to mess around. He would tell his mother he was sick with diarrhea, then have her call Coach Johns and tell him he was not feeling well.

The conversation this time was typical: "Hello, is this the coich?" She pronounced the word the way it sounded to her.

"Which coach, Ma'am?"

"The runnin' coich."

"Yes, Ma'am, this is Coach Johns."

"This heah is Miz Jackson, Streetses' mothah."

"Yes, Ma'am, Miz Jackson, how are you?"

"I tolable, coich. I know Streets suppose' to be at practice but he's feelin' poahly." Mrs. Jackson's voice carried pity in it, and by its inflection, it urged understanding. The gullible coach had a worried look on his unlined face as he asked, "What seems to be the matter with him, Miz Jackson?"

"He's runnin' off at the stummick, coich, and I 'm worried about him. You know how much I depend on Streets."

Not feeling the conversation would make the sprinter any better, Speedy needed to get back to practice. "Miz Jackson, I'm sure you know how to get him well better than I would, and I thank you for calling. I hope he gets well in a hurry."

The next day Streets showed up for practice looking pitiful. He would limp slightly, and with a desperate look, would say, "Coach, I don't think I can run today, I still feel terrible. You know how diarrhea takes it out of you."

Looking at his star sprinter, Speedy saw the occasion as the beginning of the disintegration of his track program, his season, his chance for renown. He had seen starving war prisoners who looked better than Streets Jackson as he stood there, slightly stooped, his whining voice and pained expression causing tremendous worry to this typical coach. Monday had just passed and this was gloomy Tuesday. The athletes needed to run hard today because the meet was Thursday and they took Wednesday off to rest for Thursday's meet. If he didn't work out some today, Streets would get no practice for the entire week.

Coach Johns looked at Streets. "Let's run about three easy two hundreds and call it a day." The coach didn't want to be responsible if the suffering athlete died at practice, but Streets needed some running. He dragged around the track.

On the day of the meet, Streets warmed up for the hundred meter dash with some enthusiasm, but still looked weak and pitiful when he thought Coach Johns was watching him. Inside, Streets was about to explode with laughter at the coach's concern. Actually, he felt wonderful.

When the timers and judges were ready, the dynamic sprinters lined up across the composition track in the eight brilliantly marked lanes. Each sprinter exploded out of the aluminum blocks two or three times for practice. Standing on a platform to the side and forward of the runners, the starter called through the bull horn, "Runners, take your marks."

The athletes placed their feet in the starting blocks, then wiped the grit off their hands. When they were set, the next command followed, drawn out. "Seeettt." The runners were strikingly colorful in their various two-shaded uniforms and spiked, striped shoes, their muscles bulging, with great intensity on their faces. They came up off one knee, hips raised, and as the starter's arm moved from shoulder high to straight overhead, the shot echoed from the stadium seats.

Streets Jackson was out of his blocks like a cheetah. Easily the class of the district, he flew down the precisely marked track, winning by five yards, looking like a health ad for a vitamin company.

Speedy Johns, sitting in the stands with some of his rival coaches, said to them, "I don't understand it, I thought he was sick."

One of the other coaches put his stopwatch in his shirt pocket and poked Speedy in the ribs with his elbow. "You fat little crybaby, I wish I had a couple of sick runners like that."

Streets had a chip on his shoulder as big as the grapefruit he sometimes picked, and it was as easy to knock off. He was mad at the world since there was little in his home life to make him happy. His father had stayed alive long enough to give his mother eight children by the time she was twenty-seven, then sleepily drove a loaded fruit truck in front of a freight train.

As the oldest sibling, Streets had the doubtful privilege of helping raise the other seven children. To say it did not leave him sweet and motherly would be only the edge of the truth. Like most everyone who had to be around Streets, his brothers and sisters walked a tight line.

The Jackson family had lived in several houses during Streets' nineteen years. At present, they were living in a weatherbeaten board and batten house next to the railroad embankment. The battens were pulling away from the boards and there was just a suggestion of paint left. The sheet metal roof was multicolored, rusty in places where the zinc had worn off, and the iron was oxidizing its life away. The metal roof was ugly, but it was forty years old and didn't leak, far superior to the shingle roofs of the nearby houses.

To enter the house, one stepped on a concrete block which served as steps, pushing aside a sagging door from which two jalousies were missing. The interior was furnished in the late twentieth century Good Will store motif. Sagging sofas and dining room chairs with rungs missing gave evidence of the pitter-patter and stomp-stomp of eight children. It wasn't hard to understand the doleful look in Gertrude Jackson's eyes. The two bedrooms had equal division of labor with four boys in one and four girls in the other. Gertrude slept on the sofa for privacy, if you could call it that.

Streets was bright. He had good genes and school had been easy for him, and although he had always detested homework, he was unsociable enough to be quiet in class so that he learned enough to pass without doing homework.

During his childhood, Streets' mother had worked so hard to give her family the necessities, that if she were not working on Sundays, she had no energy for church. The children did what children usually do about church when the parents don't go, they stayed home with her and got their morals from the neighborhood.

Everyone steered clear of Streets Jackson. As a festering little boy, he had hit another child without warning on the crowded school playground. It was not planned but resulted in a permanent technique with Streets. A smiling, pudgy eleven year old was in line at the water fountain when the aggressive twelve year old Streets stepped in front of Fatso. The unwise little boy said, "Hey, Streets, you git back to the end of the line, you can't butt in front of me."

Streets instantaneously slammed his fist into Fatso's jaw and the chubby child hit the ground, taking two others with him. News of Jackson's vicious act raced around the community like floodwater. From that day, Streets would hit others instantly for any reason, serious or inconsequential. People spoke to Streets carefully, and if possible, at a distance. To hit someone suddenly without warning became known as "Streetsing" someone.

As a child, Streets was aware of girls, but held them in contempt as inferior to boys. When he reached puberty, his views changed, but not to the advantage of his girlfriends, whom he always referred to as "broads." Fiercely handsome and exuding maleness, Streets continually had girls who admired him and wanted to be his woman. He learned about sex early and participated often. He saw no reason for emotional ties, and though some of his girlfriends worried themselves and their mothers for hours of which he was not aware, he truly lost no sleep over the females of the world.

Streets was honest. He would not steal, nor would he permit anyone around him to steal. When he was fifteen, one of his younger brothers told him that the thirteen year old Jonathan had stolen paper from the drug store. Streets was furious.

"Jonathan!" Streets screamed, "Did you steal some paper?"

Jonathan was so scared that he was jumping from one foot to the other. "No, Streets, Lord God no, Streets, you know I wouldn't steal no paper.."

The Jackson family cowered in the living room, away from the frightening scene in the bedroom. Gertrude Jackson did not put her nose in the thing between Streets and Jonathan. She was already afraid of the fifteen-year-old Streets. All her other children were gathered around her, deathly quiet and all eyes averted from the bedroom and from each other.

In the little, sparsely furnished bedroom, there was not much room to move with the two double beds filling up most of the space. Streets slapped Jonathan a hard blow alongside the head above the ear. The blow knocked Jonathan across one bed and onto the other. The younger boy jumped off the bed and stood whimpering, as far from his furious older brother as he could get.

Crying, Jonathan sobbed out, "Okay, Streets, okay, I did it. I need paper at school an' I did'n have no money. Please don' hit me no more."

The older boy did not plan to make this ordeal last all night as it was not his way. The time was already 11:15 and Streets wanted to go to bed. "All right, boy, you git that paper and take it back to that dollar store right now."

"You mean tonight, Streets? They ain't even open."

"I mean rat now. You run all the way down there, lay it in the door, and run back. I want to go to bed, and I won't go 'til you git back."

Jonathan grabbed the paper and headed out the hanging door, wearing nothing but cut off jeans. Barefooted, he ran down the dirt street, climbed the rock-strewn embankment to the railroad, and crossed the tracks, ignoring stones, rails and broken glass. He covered the fourteen blocks with fear inspired speed, threw the paper in the entrance to the store, and was back before Streets could get any more furious.

Streets grinned to himself as he heard Jonathan come in the door. There wasn't any stealing in the Jackson house.

# 6

# STREETS AND LATISHA

STREETS' LACK OF CARING FOR GIRLS DID NOT extend to Latisha Washington. He worshipped her. His own background and attitude were so different from the lovely cheerleader's that she seemed like an unreachable star to the gifted athlete. True to the human trait that almost everyone shows in their formative years, her unavailability made her seem ten times more desirable. He did not think of her as a sex object or plaything. If only he could date her and spend time with her, he would treat her like a pampered kitten.

On registration day, Streets found himself in line in front of Latisha. They had known each other since first grade, and were casual friends. With every hair in place as if assigned, her unblemished skin and the carefully planned wardrobe of an only child, Latisha was a striking girl.

She spoke first. "Hi, Mister America, what have you been doing for the summer?" The honey-complexioned girl spoke very carefully, pushed, prodded, propelled to perfect diction by her ambitious mother.

"I been helpin' lay microjet lines in the groves for the co-op, and I've been runnin' and pumpin' iron. What about you?"

"I've been taking a class at the community college, and working part-time in Lakeland."

Streets shifted his weight, muscles rippling with each unconscious move. "I should've known you'd be improvin' your mind," he laughed. "You never let up, do you?"

"No, I don't, and if I ever did, Mother Northella would be all over me like a swarm of blind mosquitoes." She spoke humorously but truthfully about her pushy mother.

Speaking with hope to this almost unapproachable classmate, Streets asked, "How about gettin' a coke and walking home with me when we finish registration?"

Though Latisha knew that her mother didn't want her associating very much with Streets, she had not yet been told that she could not be seen with him. "Sure, Star, maybe I can keep some other girl from capturing you on the way home." Like the other girls, she was tremendously attracted to the virile and handsome Streets, but he was strictly off limits. She said the words lightly, not meaning to encourage him.

Registration was being held in the big, air-conditioned cafeteria. A bulky, no-nonsense senior girl sat at the typing table near the entrance, a card file from each class in front of her. She was directing the loud talking students inside, allowing entrance only to the number of students the teachers could accommodate. The outside air where the students stood was cool from an early morning thunderstorm. Teachers Bruce Tucker and Caleb Johnson kept the students in line so that the process was orderly, knowing that if they didn't, the more aggressive students would have immediately broken into the front of the line. It was policed democracy.

# 7

# LATISHA'S MOTHER

LATISHA COULD TELL THAT HER MOTHER WAS angry when she hit the front door. The dark clouds emanating from the older woman's face were as foreboding as a horror movie, as threatening as a raised whip.

"The neighbors say you been walking home with Streets Jackson."

"Yes, ma'am, sometimes." Latisha was afraid of where the conversation was going.

"You know what I think of Streets. He's pure poison, Latisha, and you know I've told you to stay away from him!"

"Yes, ma'am, but...,"

"Don't but me, child. I've told you before and I'll make it so clear this time you'll think of it every morning and every night. If I see you so much as talking to Streets again, I'll lock you in your room and you won't see daylight until this time next year."

Northella Washington was laying down the law to her daughter, and although the girl knew that her mother didn't want her dating the star athlete, any slight doubt was evaporating. Her mother continued, "That boy hasn't had a good idea in his head since he was three years old." Northella was warmed to the task. "I'll not have you being serious about any boy until you get to college where you can find someone who will make you a decent husband. I haven't worked hard all these years to have you mess up your life. You may not know this, but if you start hanging around someone and dating them, whether you have anything in common with them or not, pretty soon you'll get involved. That's where babies come from." Northella was a wise woman and she knew Streets Jackson better than either Streets or Latisha could imagine. She could see it from the boy's point of view, and she knew what was going on in his head.

Two blocks away, Streets was doing some thinking on his own. He knew what the gentle people in Striptown thought of him and it was a brand which burned him. To the tough kids who were his peers, he laughed and said, "I don't give a damn what they think, they've got their noses so high in the air that they think they're better than I am. If my Daddy was still alive, we'd be one of the best families in town. You don't see those folks runnin' their mouths when I'm around. No sir. They walk wide circles around me."

Streets was right. People avoided him because he was strong and violent. He was also handsome, virile, and tremendously appealing, so that although their mothers didn't like him, many of the girls were crazy over the idea of going with him.

Streets and Latisha had three classes together. A few days after her mother's lecture, as they waited for math teacher Bruce Tucker to return from the office between classes, the striking girl leaned against a steel post which was supporting the open walkway. The sun beat down on the Saint Augustine grass and a light wind blew the red blossoms of the powder puff bushes that lined the walkway. Streets stood beside the girl, looking down at her carefully groomed hair, wishing he could touch her, but she was off limits.

"How you doing Tish?"

"Fine, Streets." The girl laughed. "You know my mother doesn't like people giving me a nickname and you're just rubbin' it in. She wants me to be Latisha and nothing else." The girl said it gently and with a smile so that Streets would know she wasn't fussing at him.

Streets laughed deeply and softly. He knew how proper Mrs. Washington was with Latisha. Everyone knew, though most thought it was presumptuous or high falootin', depending on who was doing the thinking.

"Okay, Latisha, you know I'd do anything to make you happy, you just tell me what it is. I been thinkin', pretty girl, what is it you want to do with your life, I mean after you graduate?"

"I'm going to college on a scholarship, then I'm going to become a high school math teacher." Latisha had thought this over carefully, had been pushed by her ambitious mother, and advised by the counselors. She had taken her SATs and applied for grants in aid. Her grades were exemplary and she knew she was going to college.

"Where're you going to matriculate?" He threw in the two-dollar word, knowing it would impress Latisha to some degree. As he spoke, he put his books down on the walk near the trash can. His muscles rippled with each movement, muscles that were the product of good genes, constant exercise, and the weight room. Latisha could not help but notice and it always thrilled her. In fact, being near Streets was exciting. Her biology was not all in the classroom, though she could not have put it into words. Her hormones were alive and well at Citrus City High School.

"I'm either going to Florida State or to the University at Gainesville."

Streets laughed merrily. "I'll get scholarship offers from both schools. I'll bet your mother would love it if we ended up at the same university." As he said it, a look of concern crossed the girl's face.

Three other students had come near the door to the math room, but neither group was paying attention to what the others were saying. Streets continued to speak quietly. "How come your momma don't want you goin' with me? I've never done anything to you or to her."

"My mother doesn't want me going out with anyone while I'm in high school. She's been so careful with me, and I understand even if it aggravates me sometimes. All the other girls with their babies and drugs and other problems, I don't want any of that."

Streets ducked his head at this statement. He was already a father and the girl knew it.

Latisha continued, "She doesn't want anything to stop me from climbing the highest I can. Besides, Streets, you're so rough, you hurt people and you think you can always have your own way." Latisha was one of the few people who could talk so directly to Streets and was aware that he wouldn't hold it against her.

"I wouldn't ever hurt you, Latisha." He said it in a husky voice and was very convincing. Latisha's heart thawed a little and she put her hand on the tall athlete's arm. It thrilled him, but he knew it was only a gesture.

"I'm goin' places, Latisha, and it'll be a lucky girl who goes with me. I'm goin' to make this high school football team state champions if they've got the guts to help me, and if the coaches don't screw up. Then I'm goin' to college on a football scholarship, and then play pro ball. Do you know how much they pay pro football players? You'll have to teach fifteen years to make what one of those dudes makes in one season!"

Latisha couldn't help being interested. The big football player was dynamic and intimidating. He exuded virility, and when he spoke of his ambition, he was convincing. "But what are you going to do at college?"

"Do? I'm going to play football just like I told you." Streets looked puzzled at the girl's question.

"I mean, what are you going to study?" Latisha was amazed that Streets didn't seem to have a major field of study in mind.

"Hell, Latisha, I mean heck, Latisha, that ain't important, not to a football player. They give you tutors and you don't have to take hard subjects. Anyway, they mostly go on to play pro ball, so I don't see why I need to worry about what I'll study."

Latisha looked pained. "Oh, Streets, you have to get a good education in some field. What if you don't succeed in professional football, or what if you get hurt?"

"Not a chance, baby, not a chance. You know how tough I am." There were no holes in his confidence.

There were so many girls who would have loved to be in Latisha's shoes this moment, girls who would have melted for Streets, would have done anything he asked. What he wished more than anything, was that he could have reached out to Latisha and have her hold out her arms to him, to welcome him into her embrace. He wanted to kiss those beautiful lips and crush her warm and tender body to his own, to hold her, just hold her and know that she cared for him. It wasn't a sexual thing, it was a moment of tenderness when he just wanted this most desirable of all young women to love him.

# 8

# CALEB JOHNSON

COACH CALEB JOHNSON WAS A POWERHOUSE of a man, unchanging as a big rock on the side of a mountain. At six foot eight and two eighty-five, Caleb had all the confidence born of the security that comes with being so big.

He grew up on a farm in South Carolina, one of five much-loved children, and, as he often described his brothers and sisters, "There were three boys and two girls, and each one of us was bigger than the others."

The farm didn't produce much money, only enough for security without any luxuries, but with chickens, milk cows, beef cattle, and a garden, food was plentiful.

Caleb's parents were very religious, always waiting when the little country church opened its doors. Of the five children, only Caleb was deeply spiritual. When one of his dissipating college dormitory mates asked him how he got so holy, Caleb asked him if he had time to sit down and listen. As Caleb towered over the other student, the request seemed reasonable.

"First, I want you to know I'm not holy, and I'm not good." The young giant leaned back in a massive, sturdy, older oak chair. "I go to church because I like to. I don't ever mean to act holy, and if I do, I'm sorry. I just get a good feelin' of contentment when I'm there." Caleb rose from the chair and stood in front of the dormitory window, looking out.

"How'd you get started with all that church stuff?" The smaller man looked puzzled.

"Well, it first started with my momma and daddy because they took us to the church house ev'ry time they opened the doors. They're good people and they never showed us any bad ways. Y'know, you learn what you see."

The smaller man was still puzzled. "A lot of people get carried to church. Their momma makes 'em go but that don't make 'em like it."

Caleb chuckled, "I know what you mean. I wasn't too enthusiastic about goin' to church when I was a kid, but when I was about twelve, we had a preacher who was a good man, sickly, but sincere. For several weeks in a row, he asked me to sit on the front row because he said he needed me there, that I would be a help to him, just bein' where he could talk to me. I ignored him for three or four weeks, but he kept askin' me so I finally started sittin' on the front row listenin' to him. After a while, I began to hear what he was sayin', and now I believe the Word so much that nobody could ever take it away from me."

The other student had moved from the bed to sit on one corner of a student desk in the sparsely furnished room.

Sounds of steam bumping its way through the mottled radiator interrupted the temporary quiet. The doubter was silent for an unusually long period of time. Finally, he stood up, patted Caleb on the shoulder, and left without saying another word.

At Grambling, Caleb played first team tackle on the football team for three years and playing for coach Eddie Robinson was for him an experience second to none. The coach had produced many champions and sent many players to the National Football League. His handling of the athletes and his strategy placed him among the elite in the coaching world, and he had won more games than any other coach in all of college football.

Caleb never had any doubts as to whether he should play professional football. He wanted to be a preacher and a coach, and he had no interest in money. The only way he could do both would be to take a job coaching in high school, where he could have a church in the same town. It had worked well for Caleb. He had been a force for good and he knew he was helping the young athletes.

When the new football season was starting, Caleb had much optimism about the football team and his church was running smoothly, but he was deeply concerned about the attitude of the brilliant running back, Streets Jackson. Nobody had been able to influence Streets, including Coach Johnson.

# 9

# The Season Begins

August fifteenth, ninety-eight egg-frying degrees, hotter than a leaky radiator. In central Florida, July and August were hardly the months that the chambers of commerce bragged about in their tourist brochures.

The dressing rooms at Citrus City High School were an ant bed of activity as one hundred twenty players and coaches went through the rituals necessary for the first day of football practice. They called it fall practice but the temperature was almost one hundred degrees and it would be summer until October. A coach fifteen hundred miles up the coast in Maine would roll on the floor in paroxysms of laughter to think of the Florida season as fall. Here in central Florida it was business as usual and everyone wore shorts as they had all summer.

There was a tingling air of expectancy, and you could smell victory in the air. Any college coach or recruiter would whistle if he could see the maturity and the muscular physiques of the Citrus City football players. The weight program was run by the defensive line coach and had been demanding and successful. Most of them had played football for eight years of little league, junior high, jayvees, and varsity, and it was the most important thing in their lives. The weight lifting sessions had been very successful and the muscles were bulging.

Coach Speedy Johns' track program had turned potential speed into actual mercurial speed. There was not another high school football team in Florida that could field as many athletes who could run the hundred meters under eleven seconds. To run that fast was the goal of every blossoming sprinter. Tailback Streets Jackson was the state one hundred meter champion at ten and four-tenths seconds, flanker Marty Oliver was the state high hurdles champion, linebacker Hunky King and split end Norm Tatum were the other two members of the track burning relay teams.

I was working in the equipment cage with Coach Johns and the manager, handing out shoes, shorts, and tee shirts, all that was allowable the first few days of practice. Keeping an inventory was an absolute must for us coaches, lest thousands of dollars worth of equipment end up on the streets, unavailable to the team.

Catching a short break, I looked at the bountiful crop of athletes and chuckled. I could see the bulging muscles, the cat-like coordination, and I knew we had as many veteran players as any high school football team was liable to have. Though I knew it would happen sometime, I knew of no eligibility problems.

I said to Coach Johns, "Speedy, if we can just be lucky enough not to get hit hard by injuries, we'll be the best we've ever been. We wanted to know just how good we were as coaches, and we're fixin' to find out the truth."

The mixed smell of new shoulder pads, hip pads, and shoes penetrated the heavy air as overhead fans helped the struggling air conditioning system. State rules required that there be no contact the first week, but next week we'd be in full uniform, and head knocking would begin in earnest.

# 10

# GREENWOOD

OUR TWO BANDS OF WARRIORS LOOKED ACROSS the field at each other, their faces lighted with an intensity of the moment. Only a few yards separate our two football teams as they poise for the kickoff to start the season. The scene is as old as primitive tribal warfare, and the strategy as new as bright minds can create, for this is a form of war. We coaches are the generals, the quarterbacks are our field officers, and the players running in and out of the game with instructions are our liaison.

My pregame instructions to the team are usually unemotional but specific. "Fellahs, this is the time we've been waiting for. Most of you have been playing football for years and you're good at it. When you look around at the other players, you know that you are surrounded by talent and strength. I want you to know that you are good, and you must have confidence from that knowledge. But, know this too, if you get overconfident, some team that is tough and hungry can beat you. You will play a lot of tough, hungry teams. Greenwood is a good ball team, but if we follow our game plan, we'll start the season with a win. We've gotta make Greenwood turn the ball over to us on fumbles, interceptions, and blocked punts at least three times. We must not fumble and we must not be intercepted. We've practiced protecting our punter every day, so our punts shouldn't be blocked. Receivers, run sharp patterns and remember that if your changes in direction are not sharp, the defender has a better shot at the ball than you.

I want to establish the running game, find out where their line is weakest, and not pass much in the first half. The second half, I'd like to come out throwing. Let's go blow Greenwood out of the stadium!

Greenwood won the toss and chose to receive. Flipping the coin was the best thing they did all night. Trying for a quick score, Greenwood's quarterback threw a deep pass which was batted down by our alert safety man. On second down, they ran a trap play at Horst Michler's tackle spot and the bruising Michler threw the pulling guard aside, then stopped the ball carrier for a yard loss. On third down, the Greenwood quarterback executed the draw play with finesse, but the five yards it gained still left them with fourth down and six at their own thirty-two so they were forced to punt. As precisely as Citrus City had practiced it, the Spartan punt rush broke dynamic Hunky King through the line and he blocked the punt, hitting the punter so hard that he fell five yards behind the spot he had kicked from. Guard Nels Larson recovered the ball on the Greenwood twenty-eight and the Citrus City fans rose to their feet, screaming their approval.

In the huddle, Buck Callahan looked at the ring of tense faces. "Okay, forty-six veer on two, forty-six veer on two." Streets skirted the end for five yards, then Callahan optioned to Blocker who went for four more yards, dragging the linebacker with him. On the next play, Callahan handed again to Blocker who slid off right guard for seven yards and a first down. With the ball at the Greenwood twelve, with the defense smothering Jackson and Blocker, Callahan bootlegged the ball and scored standing up. Matt Priest kicked the extra point, giving Citrus City a 7 to 0 lead.

The Spartan's confidence hung over the Greenwood team like a smothering fog as it lifted the Citrus City players to a peak of coordination and efficiency.

When Citrus City kicked off to Greenwood, the deep back brought the ball to his own thirty-five. After two plays of hammering the right side of the Spartan's unbending line, the ball was at the thirty-seven with a third and eight situation. The veteran Greenwood quarterback hit his tight end over the center for a gain of twelve and a first down. The Greenwood fans rose to their feet with a show of approval as their band broke into a militant song. In two downs, Greenwood's backs pounded at the left side for a gain of five. With a third and five, the Greenwood quarterback went to the play which had worked so well on the previous third down. He dropped back to pass, the tight end slanted over the middle, then the quarterback zipped the ball right at him. Linebacker Tony Burke saw the play developing, throwing his right hand at the ball, deflecting it up and to the left. Streets picked the ball out of the air, then collided with the intended receiver at his own forty.

My first and second team offensive guards were nearly equal so I used them to run plays into the game. A burly

Harry Little came running into the huddle as Callahan bent down on one knee.

Little's square face broke into a grin, a missing front tooth obvious when his mouth guard was out. "Coach said to run the twenty-three dive and see if they have some soft spots over there."

"Okay, twenty-three dive on one, Callahan's brittle voice clipped the words off as he spoke. The team broke from the huddle and lined up against the Greenwood defense.

Johnny Blocker was a sparkplug of a man, five foot seven and one eighty-five. He was hard to knock off his feet as his twisting, turning, gamewise running left tacklers strewn in his wake. On this play, Blocker slashed for fourteen yards and a first down. Not to be outdone, Jackson came back with eleven yards and another first down at the Greenwood twenty-nine. Callahan ran the bootleg left but there was only a two-yard gain as the defensive halfback came up fast and stopped him. Sensing that the same defensive man would again come up fast, Buck threw the lateral to Streets who streaked down the sideline only to be viciously knocked out of bounds at the Greenwood five-yard line.

We needed another touchdown so I sent in Hunky King with the instructions, "Run forty-four veer." We had been over this situation many times and I told Callahan, "On short yardage situations where it is really vital that you move the ball, run your strongest back behind your best blocking lineman." Jackson was the right back and the hulking Michler was the best lineman. On the count of one, Michler blasted aside the opposing lineman just as Jackson slammed into the hole. The inside linebacker met Streets at the opening but the powerful running back carried the defender into the end zone with frenzied force. Priest again kicked the point to make it fourteen to nothing in favor of Citrus City.

In the second quarter, the Greenwood defense stiffened, but their offense was unable to move the ball against the stingy Spartan defense.

When the second half started, we chose to receive and Marty Oliver dodged and twisted his way to the thirty-eight yard line. As I instructed, we came out passing. Buck Callahan, a senior with two previous years as a starting quarterback, had developed a passing arm second to none on the high school level. I told him to call his own plays unless I saw some weakness in the defense he didn't see, and sent in a play. Mixing his plays well, Buck threw sideline passes which were hard to defend, pulled the linebackers in with bucks in the line, then dropped the ball over their heads to the ends and the backs. He made defensive halfbacks cover deep with a decoy, then tossed the ball to the split end on a buttonhook pass in front of the defensive backs who were out of position. It was a masterful performance by a veteran, one which put points on the scoreboard. By the end of the third quarter, the scoreboard read, Citrus City 34, Greenwood 0.

I was happy the ball game was going the way we had expected. We had power, deception, and finesse, and our maturity was working in our favor.

We were two deep on both offense and defense. We were ranked third in the state preseason polls with justifiable reason. I started substituting carefully and Greenwood began to move the ball with some success, but the two touchdowns they put on the board were matched by our aggressive second-string offense.

We had one hundred forty-two musicians in our band and I was proud that we had been one of the best in Florida for years. The trumpet section, better than ever, made the grandstand rock with their sound. After each touchdown, the band played our school pep song, and on this night, they paid off for all their hot summer practices with a brilliant performance. I knew that some of the excitement that was pumping through the players was inspired by the band, though some of the team would have a hard time admitting it.

I looked down the bench and saw Franklin Powell. He was a two hundred forty pound tackle who had played for three years. Fast and strong, he had physical qualities to be an outstanding tackle, but he never tackled anyone, and he was an equally inept blocker. He was faithful at practice and was a good student, but a poor football player. As the season started, I had called Powell into what I call my plush office. I was disappointed with so much talent going to waste, doing nothing for the team, and surely discouraging the boy.

"What are we going to do with you, Powell?" You know I want to use you, but I can't stick you in the line because you don't do anything but fill up a hole."

Franklin stood there, tall, wide-shouldered, handsome, with a pleasant half smile on his face. "Well, Coach, how about tryin' me in the backfield. The reason you've always put me in the line is 'cause I'm big. I never wanted to play the line, but when I was a freshman, the line coach laughed when I told him I wanted to be in the backfield. All he ever said was that I should look in the mirror and see I was a tackle. I never said anymore to him about that. Without meaning to be disrespectful, sometimes you coaches get an idea on a player that might not be exactly right. You know you'd like to have an end that was six foot eight so he could catch passes over everybody's head, but right now our best pass catcher is only five foot six."

I sat in thought behind the old discolored oak desk in the cramped office, looking up at Powell, wondering what kind of ball carrier the young giant would make. We already had such outstanding backs, still it was a shame not to use Powell.

"Okay, Franklin, I'm going to try you at fullback behind Johnny Blocker. You sure ought to intimidate some people." I laughed when I said it.

A great look of happiness appeared on the boy's face. He was so excited he ran his words together, "Thanks Coach. I'll give it everything I've got, and you know Dad'll be proud. He's come and stood on the field every afternoon watching us, and even if he doesn't say anything, I know he's always been ashamed that I'm not one of your stars."

Now my mind was back on the ball game and I looked at the clock. With eight minutes to play, I said to Speedy, "Let's have some fun and see what Franklin Powell can do."

Coach Johns sent Powell in for Blocker. He had looked fair in practice, good enough to put in the ball game, but we still didn't know what he could do. Callahan had stayed in the game, a steadying influence on the substitutes and in the huddle he said, "Okay, Powell, how about knockin' some people on their butts. Twenty-four counter on one."

Powell took the handoff, hit the hole, and was two steps into the Greenwood backfield before the defensive halfback hit him. The one hundred seventy pound defender slowed Powell but the big ball carrier gained six yards before two more defenders cut him down. Franklin was elated when he ran back to the huddle. The other players pounded him on the back and slapped his helmet as he took his place in the ring of dirty, sweaty gridders. A rumble of approval rang through the stands. Callahan spat out the signals, "Twenty-two dive on three. Let's see if we can do it again, Franklin, break!"

Callahan put the ball in Powell's belly. The big senior bowled over the defensive end, then was gang-tackled and pounded to the ground after a gain of five and a first down at the Greenwood forty-five.

In the huddle, Callahan looked at right end Terry Foote. "Here's your chance to be a hero, Terry. We've got 'em pulled in tight and the safety is out of position. Ninety-nine post pattern on three." Foote was even with the defender before he reacted, and the end cupped his hand in front of the spiraling ball, pulling it to his side, gaining twenty yards and another first down at the Greenwood twenty-five.

On the sideline, with the outcome of the game a sure thing, I felt relaxed. I put my hand on the helmet of guard Paul Rizzo and told him, "Tell Callahan to run twenty-two option, and hurry, we don't want a delay penalty."

Center Alex Kuharski bent over the ball as Callahan rang out the signals, checking to see if the backs were lined up properly. At the count of two, our Citrus City team exploded into action, tying up one of the linebackers and the nose guard. After the handoff, a linebacker put one arm around Powell but was thrown off. Tacklers came in contact with elbows, knees, size fourteen shoes, and a staggering quantity of momentum. There was no stopping the huge Powell. He scored standing up with two players draped at different angles over his muscular body. Matt Priest kicked the extra point to make the score Citrus City 55, Greenwood 14.

I flooded the field with substitutes for the kickoff. Greenwood's deep back on the right side took the kick at the fifteen, started left, and at full speed handed off to the other deep back running right. The Citrus City substitutes, a mixture of second and third-string players, were slow to react to the handoff and the Greenwood ball carrier raced to his own forty-three before being pulled down by two frenzied Spartan tacklers. In the short time left, the Greenwood quarterback moved his team smoothly down the field, scoring as the final whistle blew. Franklin Powell's father ran out of the grandstands, jumped the short chain link fence separating the spectators from the field, then ran over to me. "What'd you think of my boy, Coach?" The man was so happy and excited that I was somewhat amused, but I knew the deep pleasure the senior Powell was feeling.

"Mister Powell, if I were any happier, I'd be jumping fences too. It's a great night for you and Franklin and for the team. I just hope we're that good against Ocean City."

# 11

# GAME TWO
# OCEAN CITY

THE NOISE IN OUR DRESSING ROOM WAS SO loud it was hard to be heard above the din as the players were excited beyond a level they would admit. Football had become their life, more important than passing grades, girlfriends, cars, or any other thing in their lives. The first thing they thought of in the morning and the last thing at night was the hope for a state championship.

Streets Jackson had a superstition that if he were the last player whose ankles were taped, he would star again and true to the cantankerous player's wishes, the trainer was taping him last.

We coaches had our heads together, quietly discussing strategy for the game.

I walked out of the equipment cage. Tonight our

coaching staff was wearing neat white duck pants and new red sports shirts with the words Citrus City Coaching Staff printed in white above the pocket. We also wore a red and white cap with CC stamped above the bill. I raised my arms and shouted above the din, "Fellahs, let me have your attention!" I shouted it twice and someone whistled loudly before the cool cement block room quieted enough so I could be heard.

"Men," (I hesitated to call them men because many were still childlike in many ways.) "Tonight is a new ball game. We beat Greenwood and it was a great way to start the year, but this is a different game. Coach Johnson is going to give you some instruction before we go out there."

Caleb Johnson towered over everyone and moved among the players as he spoke.

"You'd better pay attention to what Coach Warren said to you, this is a new ball game." Coach Johnson's deep bass voice reflected the sounding board that was his huge body. "Ocean City is better than Greenwood. From last Monday's scouting report, you know they are tough up the middle on both offense and defense. They're a little bit slow but they're big. You won't push 'em around, so if they stop us part of the time, don't panic. We're faster than they are and we're just as big, and we're going to win the ball game. We'll set up the wall to the right on the kickoff the first time we receive so let's make that go right and everything else will fall in place. How about it Coach Johns, d'you want to add anything?"

"Thanks, Coach, just this: You'll hear it every time we play. We can't stand any fumbles or interceptions, and let's don't get any punts blocked."

"Coach Warren?" Caleb Johnson nodded and waited for me to speak.

"Let's have our team prayer." Because of the diversity of belief and non-belief, prayer was not acceptable at all the high schools across the nation. Here in the deep south Bible Belt, prayers were generally accepted, and those who were indifferent went along with the crowd.

Coach Johnson, half teacher, half preacher, and surely one hundred percent both, knew what he believed. He prayed, "Our Father, we thank you for giving us strong, healthy bodies and good minds. We pray that we will use them to your glory. We pray for Your protection and the grace to use what You have given us the best way we can. In all things we praise You. Amen."

A clamor came from the throats and cleats of the Spartan team as they ran single file from the door of the dressing room, under the goal posts and through the paper wall held by the cheerleaders. The Citrus City crowd thundered its approval. In this football-loving town, the game was the high point of the week for most everyone.

Horst Michler, Hunky King, and Streets Jackson met the Ocean City captains and the officials in the center of the field. The referee flipped a silver dollar and Hunky King opted for tails, winning the toss.

"We'll receive." King's alert eyes looked through the posts of his gray face guard.

The referee looked at the Ocean City captain. "Which goal do you want to defend?" There was almost no wind so the choice was not very important. The Ocean City captain looked up at the flag to see which way it was blowing.

"We'll kick from that end," the captain said as he pointed to the north end of the field.

When the referee moved to the south and indicated that Citrus City had won the toss, a roar of approval rang from the stands. The Spartans lined up with Streets Jackson on the left side of his ten yard line and Marty Oliver on the right side, opposite Streets. The Ocean City kicker boomed the ball end over end, straight at Oliver, and Marty had to retreat slightly to get it. He took one step forward, then started left. The flow of Ocean City tacklers started to their right to get Oliver. The game-wise Streets Jackson, sure of himself, thought instantly it looked good. Jackson sprinted to his right meeting Oliver and taking the handoff as the Citrus City players began to form a protective wall near the right sideline. Streets was the right ball carrier to make the play work. The realization of the handoff hit the onrushing Ocean City players and they changed direction to get the champion sprinter, but their reaction was a split second late.

We had spent more time than usual on the sideline kickoff return. There was so much to cover at practice, yet we hoped we were justified in practicing the wall. With our superb backfield speed, it was a good gamble.

A defensive player got an arm on Jackson just as he reached the corner to turn up the sideline but Hunky King blocked the Ocean City player at the same instant, springing Streets free. From there to the goal line, seventy yards away, it was all Streets, his blazing speed daring Ocean City and the whole world.

His figure was a blur of red and white as fingers and hands grabbed at him in vain. Streets high-stepped the last twenty yards, raising his arms and face to the sky in exultation. Priest missed the extra point which disturbed me a little. More than that, I couldn't help but frown because I knew it would be a season long problem to fight overconfidence.

On the following kickoff, Priest booted a high, end over end ball to the Ocean City deep back on the twelve yard line. The Ocean City team massed in the center to block for the ball carrier, knocking two Citrus City tacklers off their feet at the twenty. The ball carrier burst through the hole and slashed his way to the forty before he was dropped to the ground with a grinding tackle by Marko Parelli.

In the defensive huddle, Hunky King passed my instructions to the defense. Hunky told them, "Auburn defense, and you linebackers sock it in there tight."

The Ocean City play started out looking like a run, then the quarterback suddenly shot a pass to his fullback who had spurted through the line to circle behind the Spartan linebackers. The play was good for a gain of eleven yards. First and ten at the Citrus City forty-nine. The strain was stamped on the faces of the lineman as they glared each other across the line of scrimmage.

I watched the Ocean City huddle, wondering what they would come up with. At the line of scrimmage, there was an unusually long count and Nels Larson jumped offside at the count of three, knocking down an Ocean City lineman and drawing penalty flags from all the officials. The referee marched off the five-yard penalty to put the ball on our forty-four. Two running plays netted them six yards and a first down at our thirty-eight.

The Ocean City split end ran straight at Morton, our left defensive back. Morton took three steps backward and their receiver suddenly stopped and took a pass right in front of him, catching the ball on the thirty. Streets lowered the boom on the receiver, hitting him so hard that the boy lay on the turf for a brief time before staggering to his feet. Ocean City called time out and the quarterback ran over to the bench.

The Ocean City coach stood eye to eye with his quarterback, giving him directions for the next play. Returning to the field, the quarterback pitched to his tailback who was running wide. It was good for three yards, down to the Spartan twenty-seven. On the pass play which followed, the split end headed straight at Morton again. This time, rather than retreat, Morton played the end close, expecting another short pass, and as he crowded the potential receiver, the end first hooked, then released downfield, and as he did, Morton stumbled. The end broke into the clear, caught the pass at the twelve and crossed the goal line and Streets cut him down as if he were swinging a scythe.

This time the end did not get up. He lay there motionless and the officials called for the team doctor. The doctor and the trainer hurried to the end zone, and as they bent over him the player began to move his arms and legs. A sigh of relief could be heard from the stands. In a moment, when the doctor and the trainer helped him to his feet, they moved him on unsteady feet to the sideline. Streets stood in the back of his huddle grinning.

The Ocean City extra-point try flew to the left of the goalpost and the official's hands moved to the side of his body, signaling no good. The score stood 6 to 6 and our coaching staff breathed easier. Even though we felt our team to be superior, the early tie in the ball game made us anxious.

I told the team to run the wall again on the kickoff, only there would be no handoff. Maybe that would fool some of the Ocean City players.

The booming kick backed Oliver to the five. Again he started left, faking the handoff to Streets who was heading for the right sideline and Jackson's fake pulled some of the defense with him. Oliver scooted left carrying the ball to our thirty-seven before he was knocked down.

On first and ten, Callahan pitched to Oliver but the play was good for only one yard. No doubt about it, Ocean City was not intimidated by our reputation. Callahan handed off to Blocker and their big inside linebacker dropped him at the Citrus City forty-one after a gain of three. Callahan broke the huddle and the Spartan team took their positions. At the count of one, Callahan faked a handoff to Blocker, started down the line, and as the linebacker charged him, Callahan pitched to Streets who tore down the field for eleven yards. On first and ten Callahan threw a pass to split end Norm Tatum but a defender broke it up.

Fullback Blocker surged through the line for four yards to the Ocean City forty-four, then Callahan called for the quick pitch to Jackson. Before the huddle broke, the arrogant Jackson said, "It's about time, man. Watch my smoke." True to his word, Jackson's speed was too much for the defenders and he raced into the end zone, covering the forty-four yards like a race horse. What Jackson didn't see was the penalty flag thrown by the umpire when Terry Foote clipped an Ocean City player far upfield from the speeding Jackson. It was a senseless blocking attempt and couldn't have helped the ball carrier, even if it had been legal.

Streets was furious when he came back to the huddle. "Which one of you sonsabitches clipped on my run?" Nobody said anything and Callahan called for the same play.

After the clip, the ball was on the Citrus City forty-one. Streets took the pitchout, stiff-armed a charging linebacker, and outran the safety man, scoring again. Two plays, two touchdowns, and the Citrus City stands were in bedlam. I could see the Ocean City's head coach who stood on the sidelines, head down in shock and disbelief. He must have known there was almost no defense against such talent. The kick was good and the scoreboard read, Citrus City 13, Ocean City 6.

Jackson scored twice more, once on a fourteen yard run, and to prove his versatility, once going very high in the air to catch a pass, then outrunning the Ocean City secondary to put another TD on the board. Ocean City scored again, but it wasn't enough and the score ended Citrus City 27, Ocean City 13.

As they walked off the field together, Hunky King said to Streets, "You played a fine ball game buddy! You won that game for us."

Streets replied, "What'd you expect Hunky, I was the best thing on the field."

The Citrus City Herald's account of the game on the front page read:

STREETS JACKSON RUNS WILD

> In the game with Ocean City, the Spartan foes discovered more than they wanted to know about Streets Jackson. The speedy Jackson, reigning one hundred meter dash champion, ran around and through the Ocean City Eagles, knocking them from the list of unbeaten teams, putting himself in solid contention for all-state honors.
>
> While the rest of the Spartans were held to reasonable gains by the strong Ocean City team, Jackson scored four times. A preview of things to come was given by the talented halfback on the opening kickoff when he went eighty-five yards to score, virtually untouched. Twice the Eagles had answered the Spartan's touchdowns, each time seeming to gain momentum and looking like Citrus City's equal. Following Jackson's touchdown on the kickoff, Ocean City came back with a determined move down the field, mixing their plays well, and

passing for a touchdown. Jackson's second score was even more spectacular because he had to score it twice. He ran the ball in from the forty-four and the play was called back for clipping. Just to show that he wanted to score to stay on the scoreboard, on the next play, Jackson went fifty-nine yards for the TD.

Ocean City answered with another pass for a touchdown, this time for forty yards. The third quarter saw the two teams move the ball back and forth between the thirty yard lines. In the fourth quarter, Jackson ran wild, moving the ball almost at will. He scored on a fourteen yard burst up the middle, and with two minutes to go, added an insurance touchdown with a pass from Callahan. Matt Priest scored the extra points. Next week, the Spartans travel to Valley to take on the Grenadiers.

An interesting and encouraging development in the Citrus City offense is the duel that is developing between dependable Johnny Blocker and Franklin Powell at the fullback slot. Powell was moved from tackle to fullback to take advantage of his size and speed. Blocker, a veteran fullback, has been one of the main cogs in the Spartan offense. Powell's very evident power has made a real battle between the two for that position. We'll be fascinated to see who ends up in the first team spot.

# 12

# Coach Warren's Postgame Party

Twenty-seven to thirteen. Twenty-seven to thirteen! As I drove toward home after the game, I slapped my knee in delight at the victory, I couldn't help it. Another tough team out of the way.

I had seen the last player gone from the dressing room, Doc Whitman had examined the injuries, the dirty red and white uniforms were being washed by the managers, and I was headed home for the party. It would be a sumptuous buffet as always. After each home game, one of the coaches' wives entertained with a gourmet feast and all the ladies who came brought special dishes.

The party would be attended by all who were closely associated with the Citrus City Athletic Department plus the school administrators and close friends of the coaches.

There was a certain amount of local prestige to be derived from being included in a postgame party in this football town.

I parked my four-year-old Chevy in the uncluttered carport. Blackie met me at the door and threw her arms around me. She said, "How's the greatest coach in the South?"

"How about the luckiest coach in the South?" I knew I was thorough and knowledgeable, but I couldn't brag about myself when I knew how lucky I was to have so much talent on the team and so far, no bad injuries.

"Okay, Lucky, it surely looked good to the Citrus City fans."

"Any victory looks good to the fans. That was a tough ball game and I'm glad it's over." I paused for a moment and looked into the eyes of this beautiful, uncomplicated woman that I loved. I hugged her again, and then said, "How about a coke?"

Blackie laughed at me and said, "Boy you know how to ruin a romantic moment, don't you?"

A murmur of happy women's voices came from the kitchen and the long living room. In the TV room, some of the coaching staff were already gathered, dissecting the game.

I could hear basketball coach Tom Hartz, always an optimist, who had the floor. "We're going all the way 'cause I don't see a team on our schedule that can stop us. Some of these schools have our size but nobody has our speed and balance."

Sitting in a straight-backed chair, legs around the back of the chair, hands on top, Speedy laughed at Coach Hartz. "Boy, I wish you were coaching the next six games; I like your attitude. I sure hope you're right because that ball game tonight was a booger. Ocean City forgot to roll over and play dead and I don't think they read our clippings."

Coach Hartz would not be dissuaded, "Yeah, but with people like Streets Jackson and Callahan and Michler, we're gonna win 'em all."

Coach Caleb Johnson came through the front door, his six foot eight height exactly fitting the door frame, a happy smile on his face. His wife, Sandra, met him at the door. "How's the best coach in the South?"

Blackie overheard Sandra saying exactly what she had just said and smiled at me.

"Don't hang that on me," the big man said, "I've got all the problems I can handle."

Guests were coming in a constant, colorful stream. The sounds of the voices were becoming louder as the crowd increased. People carrying plates heaped with food looked for places to sit and there was an air of happiness, a light-hearted feeling born of the victory.

We coaches had worked thousands of hours to reach this point. We had played college football, taken classes in coaching methods, read dozens of books, and coached for years. We had researched birth certificates, suffered players injuries, lost players to ineligibility, had seen some boys with great physical ability and no heart fail for us, and had seen some poor physical specimens win for us with great effort. To have a state championship contender was no fluke. We had earned it.

Blackie drifted back to the kitchen to see that the food was well arranged on the buffet tables.

I went into the larger, quieter living room to eat, and a striking young blonde came and sat next to me in my quiet corner. With patrician beauty fit to grace a palace, she was stunning in a black velour dress and I breathed a little sigh as she greeted me. Beth Hagman was every man's favorite but was held at arms length by the women. She was just too perfect. She was an elementary school teacher, gregarious and happy, soft and charming.

"Hi, handsome. How's my favorite coach?"

"Fine Beth, how's the pretty girl?" We had come to Citrus City the same year. We had become friends and had a warm, relaxed relationship, or so I thought.

Beth's answer startled me. "I'd be better, Angus, if you'd pay more attention to me." It was said earnestly, and in quiet confidence.

"Honey, if I paid attention to you, I'd lose my happy home."

"We could make beautiful music together, Angus. You don't know how much I have to share." Beth's perfectly formed lips and impeccable complexion made her radiantly appealing.

I realized that she wasn't saying this lightly. She looked at me expectantly, waiting for me to say more. I knew that I appealed to some women, but I certainly wasn't looking for any outside romance. I said, "Beth, you're a lovely girl and I like you. If I weren't married, and if there were no Blackie, I'd camp on your doorstep. I'd be a fool if I said you didn't charm me like you charm most every man around you, but I love Blackie so much and I'm so happy with her that neither you nor any woman can cause me to do anything that would hurt my wife."

I touched the lovely girl on the cheek as I said, "Our married life has been full of contentment. I can be away from the house every afternoon or up in Gainesville or Tallahassee watching ball games, and I don't worry about what my wife is doing. If she says she's going to Orlando to shop, I know that's exactly what she's doing. She knows I'm doing exactly what I tell her, and this makes me a better person and a better coach. I can look athletes in the eye and know they trust me. There's nothing in our lives that isn't what it appears, and if you and I messed around, we'd both suffer, both become less than we are." Tears appeared in the corner of Beth's eyes as I continued. "I like you pretty girl, so let's leave it that way."

I took my half full plate into the room where the ball game was being replayed by the grandstand quarterbacks.

Math teacher Bruce Tucker, who served as assistant track coach, called out to Speedy, "Hey, Speed, what'd you think of Streets tonight?"

The always excitable Coach Johns' eyes lit up. "Wasn't he awesome? Four TD's!! Without him we might've been up a creek. I believe he's got first team all-state in his pocket." The tall, almost gaunt Tucker pushed his rimless glasses up the bridge of his nose. "How come our other backs couldn't move the ball?"

Coach Johns winced at the remark. He was proud of his backfield and took the criticism as a slur, not serious, but biting, nevertheless. "First of all, that was a tremendously talented football team we played, one of the five best in Florida. Also, it wasn't that the other backs couldn't move the ball, they were making three or four yards on most plays, and if Streets hadn't been there, we could still have made the offense go. Streets just played like a wild man and what he did tonight made everyone else look bad."

The assistant track coach wanted some credit for the blue chip athlete's success. "Those two twenties and four forties in track sure didn't hurt him."

"That's the truth." Speedy's eyes took on a new sparkle as he thought of the influence his track program had on his running backs. The two track coaches had drawn aside from the other men who were gathered in small groups, discussing the football season. At five eight and one seventy-five, the thirty-five-year-old Johns was starting to put on a little belly. He had been a game breaker as a halfback in college, given to the spectacular play. When he had gone into a ball game, his adrenaline level was always so high that he could be counted on for something special, an interception, the catch of a critical pass, the perfect running of the coach's pet play of the week. Even though he was not in top condition, Speedy could still outrun all the backfield on the Citrus City team except Jackson.

Full of enthusiasm, Coach Johns was a favorite of everyone. He said, "You know, Bruce, when I was in high school, I thought the speed a runner was born with was all he ever had. I didn't believe you could make him faster by practice, but we've proved that athletes do get faster. We both know you can't make a slow guy fast, but you can make any athlete somewhat faster with concentrated practice. If Streets can't run a hundred meters in ten three, I'm Jesse Owens."

Caleb Johnson's booming bass laugh sounded through the room. "You don't look much like Jesse Owens to me." Peals of laughter followed the remark.

I sat next to Caleb. To be around the line coach was to be calm because he spread oil on the waters and made everyone feel good. "How'd you feel about the ball game, Caleb?"

The big man looked thoughtful, his brow creased with a frown. "I'm happy we won, Angus, but I'm disturbed, too. They never should have scored twice on us. We've got to work on pass defense and we've gotta practice movin' the ball in short yardage situations. We've either got to make Stone better on pass defense or replace him. More than anything else, I'm really worried about Streets. He's mad at the world and he thinks he's the only good ball player we've got. You know his daddy got killed when he was a little boy and he's had to help his mother raise all those children, and he hates it. He has a bright future but he's so doggone filled with anger that he can't see what's gonna happen tomorrow, and I guarantee he'll make trouble for us before the season is over."

# 13

# Game 5
# Dover

We were powerful and undefeated, ranked number two in the state polls. The next opponent was to be Dover, and almost every other team had beaten Dover like an old piano. I was deeply worried. How do you get a team up psychologically to play such an opponent? Dover's one win was a fluke, seven to six victory over an equally inept team, but we always had to remember that on every team there is some exceptional talent. It may be hidden by inexperience, lack of depth, or poor coaching, but it's always there, waiting to strike you. To our coaching staff, Dover was a rattlesnake waiting to strike.

The newspapers had been more than generous and all the Spartan athletes had scrapbooks full of laudatory clippings. The week of practice was very good and there were no significant injuries. With our unmatched speed, the offense was running its plays better than anytime during the year. The timing was so good that Coach Johns said he didn't see how we could improve on it.

The Orlando Sentinel had done a special on Citrus City the past weekend, and the photographers used up an hour of valuable practice time on Monday. Our coaches felt that with our weakest opponent coming up, this was the most opportune time to do it. I hated to see the Sentinel pour so much praise on so many players.

I looked at the clippings and complained to Blackie, "If we have anyone who hasn't had the bighead before, the Sentinel took care of that for us. They made these kids look like All-Americans."

In the unfamiliar visitor's dressing room under the Dover stadium, our players were noisier than usual. They laughed and kidded each other and there was some unusual horseplay. On this late October evening, a chill emanated from the bare concrete floors and walls, and I felt a different chill.

I could guess what was going on over in the Dover dressing rooms. They had a first year coach, hired to prop up a sagging football program and he had met with very little success, but his kids liked him and believed in him. He was trying to install a new offense and defense with a small turnout of players and that's not what champions are made of. I knew they had one player I wish I had. McLaren, at five eleven and one ninety-five, was fast, dynamic, and terribly strong. He was the county weightlifting champion and was an all-purpose defensive back.

Before we went on the field, I commanded the teams attention. "If you guys are taking this Dover team lightly, you're making a bad mistake. We know they've won only one game, but remember, I told you before the first game that if you let up, some tough team could beat you. This bunch is tougher than you know. Their coach knew when the season started that he might not win many games using his seniors, so he's gone with the younger, more talented players, looking forward to better teams in the future. They have played five games and it's about time they put it all together." Out of the corner of my eye, I caught Johnny Blocker wink at Parelli who put his hand over his mouth to hide a smile.

We won the toss and chose to receive. As my boys sat on their haunches, dreaming of the victories, the Dover kicker made a perfect onside kick and recovered his own kick at our forty-one. I covered my eyes as the Citrus City spectators grunted their displeasure.

The first play from scrimmage, the Dover right half sliced through for six yards to our thirty-five. Coach Caleb Johnson signaled a change of defense to Hunky King but it wasn't much help as Marko Parelli jumped offside to give Dover a first down at our thirty. The Dover quarterback dropped back to pass and the eager, hard-charging Spartan linemen overran him and the quarterback sprinted up the middle to the eighteen. Nobody in the stadium could believe it. The spectators on the Dover side were all standing, screaming encouragement to the team they had seen lose so often.

In the quiet Citrus City grandstand, Franklin Powell's father said to his football buddy, Lowell Foote, "What the devil's going on out there, Lowell? They can't move the ball like that on us!"

Lowell Foote, digging into a bag of peanuts, looked sideways at Powell. "I know they can't but they are." Then he screamed at the top of his voice. "Get in the ball game! Wake up out there!"

On the next play, first and ten at the eighteen, the Dover

quarterback threw a high, looping pass toward the split end in the end zone. Streets and Morty Stone, overeager to stop the Dover offense, converged on the end, knocking him down before the pass got to him. As the penalty flag from the nearby official flew into the air, the ball, batted upward by Jackson, fell into the arms of the Dover end. The official's arms signaled touchdown and Dover's three thousand ecstatic fans made an uproar that sounded like ten thousand.

The Dover kicker sent the ball booming through the uprights, but he didn't have time to enjoy it as a furious Streets Jackson barreled into him, knocking him down, drawing a rain of penalty flags. Madder than ever, the volatile Jackson smashed his helmet to the ground, breaking the faceguard.

On the Dover sideline, the coach could be seen talking earnestly to his defensive captain and pointing at Jackson. I knew what he was saying, even though I was sixty yards away. "You see what I mean about Jackson's temper?"

"Yes sir! He's already so mad he can't think."

"Okay, son, let's go after him!"

We were penalized fifteen yards on the ensuing kickoff for Jackson's unsportsmanlike conduct. Kicking from our forty-five, the Dover kicker's spirited boot carried into the end zone where Jackson hauled it in, hesitated, then started straight up the middle. It was a mistake and Streets was pounded to the ground by the muscular McLaren and five other adrenaline-high players at our ten yard line.

Callahan didn't realize that Streets was too furious to think straight. He faked to Blocker then sprinted down the line, and as the defensive end closed in on him, he pitched to Jackson. The ever present free safety McLaren raced up to smash Streets at the line of scrimmage. Two more Dover players gang-tackled Streets before he went down, mad and confused. The play was good for one yard and put the ball on our eleven yard line. After our team dragged up to the line of scrimmage, Callahan handed off to Blocker who could gain only two yards. A disgusted Dewey Thomas mouthed off in the huddle, "What's the matter with you ball carriers? We're workin' our butts off, makin' holes for you and you're not doin' anything!"

The cool Callahan said, "Okay, knock it off. It won't do any good to holler at each other, so let's play ball." He hesitated a moment to get a message from the bench.

I sent in Bernie Little with instructions for Callahan. "Coach says to run the counter-option."

Buck faked to Jackson, then pitched to Blocker running left. The play was good for twenty-two yards and we breathed a premature sigh of relief. On the next play, Callahan faked to Blocker driving off left tackle, then shot a pass to Jackson who had rounded left end. When Streets turned around, the pass was almost in his face and he caught it just in time to be slammed into by several zealous Dover tacklers.

McLaren hit Jackson late, and it was more than the temperamental running back could stand. As McLaren leered at him, Jackson's fist came around in a looping punch, knocking him to the ground. The nearby official threw a flag, then escorted Jackson to our bench where he told me, "Coach, I'm putting this player out of the game for fighting." Naturally, I was stunned. We were playing terribly and my best running back was being thrown out of the game.

I couldn't blame the official, and the blow was so obvious to the spectators that there was no doubt about what had happened.

With Streets out of the ball game, I thought the team might settle down and play ball, but it had the opposite effect and Dover played like a team possessed. They stopped our offense and we had to turn the ball over to them on a punt. They started pecking away at our defense, gaining a few yards at a time on line plays, short passes, and end runs. Just when it looked as if they were stopped after two downs, they would come up with some play to gain enough for a first down. Before the half, they scored again and our team, sound asleep on their feet, couldn't come our of their daze. Our normally potent backfield, without the prop Jackson gave them, couldn't move the ball. Of course, there was more to it than our overconfidence; after a poor season's start, Dover was starting to mature and we just happened along at the wrong time.

Oliver was good for a few yards at a time, but Blocker, so sure of himself before the game started was shut down completely. The half ended with the score: Dover 13, Citrus City 0.

I didn't like to get too emotional at halftime, and normally wouldn't be sarcastic, but I couldn't restrain myself. When I had the team in the dressing room, I told them, "I have some of the newspaper clippings you've been reading, about how great the Citrus City football team is. Would you like for me to read them to you? You were truly magnificent. Why, in the first half you were getting beat by two touchdowns by the worst team in the district. By acting like a spoiled brat, Jackson's been kicked out of the game, and I would like for someone to tell me what he thinks of the pushovers now. I'll tell you what I will do, I'll give you a preview of what the Orlando newspapers will say tomorrow morning! They'll tell how on Friday night in a stunning upset, the formerly powerful Citrus City Spartans were pushed all over the field by a heads up Dover team, and the news report will continue like this. Everybody on the Citrus City team shared in the loss. The big defensive line couldn't stop the Dover offense and the lightning fast backs were as flat as a snail's belly. They couldn't get out of their own way, and to make matters worse, Streets Jackson got thrown out of the game for fighting!

"I hope you boys will enjoy reading that because that's what you'll see.

"The second half, I'm going to start the second team on both offense and defense. Maybe a little rest will help you guys on the first team get your act together."

True to my word, I sent the second team defense in to kick off to Dover, and it worked like a charm. The kick flew end over end to the waiting return man at the ten and he made it back only to the twenty-two before a swarm of eager Spartan substitutes wrestled him to the turf. The Dover team moved the ball, but their former edge was gone, blunted by the enthusiasm of our second team. After one struggling first down, Dover ran three more plays, gaining only four yards, and were forced to punt from their own thirty-eight. The low, line drive punt carried only to our forty where an alert and happy Bunky Pitts gathered the ball in on a dead run and took it back to the Dover forty-five before being cut down by a Dover tackler. Pitts was not as big or as fast as his much publicized teammates, but he was faithful and experienced, in ecstasy to be in the ball game in place of Marty Oliver. Pitts' behind had enough splinters from riding the bench that he could sell cordwood.

I sent Buck in with the second team offense, feeling that we needed the stability that his experience would give the team. Powell, relieved of playing tackle, was like a little kid with a new toy, and he took over Blocker's slot at fullback. Jackson's substitute, Benny Wells, was running tailback.

At the sideline, Speedy Johns talked earnestly to me, scratching his fanny to the delight of some of the fans and the chagrin of others. He told me, "I'm sure glad we gave

Franklin some playing time in the early ball games. He'll come through, watch what I say."

No sooner were the words out of Speedy's mouth than Powell tore through the line with a Dover lineman and a linebacker clinging to him, but they could not stop him before he had gained five yards. Callahan mixed the plays well, throwing passes and running Wells and Pitts. For the most part, our offense had to grind it out, getting a few yards at a time as the Dover team had been doing the first half. The two teams dueled back and forth between the thirty-yard lines, neither able to score. Our punter had to kick three times in the third quarter, more than he had punted all season.

During a time out, I called Franklin Powell over to the bench. "Franklin, we've got to pull this ball game out of the fire, and you may be the only one who can do it. Go back in there and tell Buck I said to run twenty-four counter."

Powell was one of those wide-eyed believers who didn't need to analyze someone's emotions or hidden meanings. When I said, "You may be the only one who can do it," that was good enough for Franklin. On the play, he banged through the hole, knocking the linebacker over as if he were a bowling pin. The play was good for eight yards. It became a game to Powell as he was gang-tackled by McLaren and the stubborn Dover defense.

Callahan kept calling Powell's plays and the big fullback continued biting off chunks of yardage. The more the Dover team piled on him, the more Franklin reveled in it. Our spectators were caught up in the excitement of his hour of challenge, and they began to scream encouragement to him and the team. With eight minutes to go in the fourth quarter, Franklin burst across the goal line for our first score to make it Dover 13, Citrus City 6. Matt Priest ran on the field to attempt the extra point. Like almost everything else the first team had done all night, the try for point was no good. The spectators and our coaching staff felt the cold chill of a loss closing in on us. Only eight minutes left, we were kicking off to Dover, and it would take eight points to beat this underdog team that had suddenly become the unbeatable foe.

Dover clung tenaciously to the lead, driving the ball to our twenty-four before they ran out of steam. I had to give our substitutes credit because they fought like their lives depended on the game. With a little less than two minutes to go, we took possession of the ball with seventy-six yards to go.

"Give the ball to Powell!! Give the ball to Powell!!" I could hear the crowd yelling, but I didn't really need their advice because that's exactly what I meant to do.

I told Callahan, "Give the ball to Powell every time you can." Powell responded by surging up the field for eight yards on the first down play, carrying Dover's purple and white jerseyed players with him as he went. With second and two on the thirty-two, Callahan threw a sideline pass to Pitts, good for seven yards, stopping the clock as he stepped out of bounds. With only one minute left, from our thirty-nine, Callahan ran the hurry up offense, calling Powell's play from the line of scrimmage. The strapping senior couldn't be stopped until he carried the ball fourteen yards for a first down at the Dover forty-seven.

When the officials moved the chains, it gave us a break on the clock. The sideline pass to Wells was batted down by an alert outside linebacker, but it also stopped the clock with thirty-eight seconds left.

As he lined the team up, Callahan saw how close to the line the defensive backs were playing, with the safety man moved over a bit to the left, in a position to stop Powell at the spot he had been hitting. Why Dover was using the defense they were was a mystery to us. Callahan audibled a pass on a quick count, and as he backed up, he saw the safety had stayed with Benny Wells over the middle. Right end Charles Hooper headed straight at the defensive halfback, and as he neared the defender, Hooper cut right about four yards with the defender following his move. Then Hooper cut back toward the goal post nearest him. He had caught only three passes during the season, but he didn't have time to think about success or failure on this one. Callahan shot the pass at him like a fastball over home plate and the end smothered it into his arms. The frustrated defender tackled Hooper but not before he had made twenty-six yards and a first down at the Dover twenty-one. While the officials were moving the chains, Callahan lined the team up, ready to go with twenty-five seconds left in the game.

When the Dover secondary loosened up to prevent the long pass for the score, Callahan gave the ball to Powell. Not wanting to leave the scoring to someone else, Franklin tore down the field like a rhinoceros, not stopping until he ran out the back of the end zone. The Citrus City fans yelled and threw their programs in the air, knowing a tie was probable and a win possible.

For the first time on this cool Friday evening, the band sounded like they were at the state band contest.

I was busy on the sideline, talking to Caleb and Speedy Johns because I needed their advice on this decision. We three, facing each other in a small circle, said almost in unison, "Run Powell for two points!"

We laughed but we didn't fool around. Callahan was at the sideline to be sure there weren't any mistaken messages. When Dover saw that we were not lined up to kick the point, they set their defense to stop Powell because they knew he was coming. It did no good. Powell had enough adrenaline flowing in his veins to fill a pint jar, and he blasted the defenders aside, scoring two points to win the game for us.

# 14

# NATALIE SHIRES

IT WAS THE SECOND COACHES' PARTY OF THE season and Natalie Shires sat in the corner, a situation to which she was accustomed. At age thirty-five, Natalie knew the bloom was gone. With cascades of brown hair, brown eyes, full lips and just slightly larger than normal nose, Natalie was attractive, but she was no sexpot. The much talked about Friday night postgame party was the most exciting thing that had happened to Natalie since her arrival in Citrus City. She sat alone, musing over the events which brought her to this night.

Born in Toledo, Ohio, the last of three children, she was raised by a stern, Victorian mother and a kind, easygoing father. Her father had died during Natalie's last year of college, and she sometimes thought he did it to escape the sharp tongue of her mother. In college, Natalie was not a sorority member. Since she commuted and was a serious student, her social life was almost nil. When her father became ill, Natalie gave as much time to him as her studies would allow.

Without any serious boyfriends, Natalie graduated from college unsought after and virginal. There was a very small pension from her father that helped pay the bills after her father's death, but Natalie was forced to support her mother. She took a teaching job in a girls' school in Toledo, and there spent ages twenty-two to thirty-four honing her teaching skills and pulling more from her students than they wanted to give. Miss Pemberton's Preparatory School for young ladies was not a great place to meet men. In those twelve years, Natalie had several dates without the knowledge of her dictatorial mother, but never found anybody she wanted to run away with.

When Natalie's mother, Amanda, decided she would like to move to Florida to escape the Ohio winters, Natalie was thrilled. The demands of her job and her mother kept Natalie from trying to find a man. The years passed so quickly she was amazed when her thirty-fourth birthday rolled around.

The Shires' home in Toledo sold for as much as Amanda asked, but less than it was worth. She was not going to become wealthy buying and selling real estate. They bought a neat doublewide mobile home in Lake Honey Mobile Home Park near Citrus City, listed in the brochure as a "Sweet Place to Live."

Central Florida was hotter than either Natalie or Amanda realized it would be in the summer, but they were intrigued by the change in their lifestyle. Natalie swam in the Lake Honey pool and her mother became involved in the round robin bridge league. In fact, the social activities of the Lake Honey senior citizens kept Amanda so busy that Natalie was able to sit back and take a look at her social life. She saw that unless there were a miracle, or she became more aggressive, she might very well go through life as an old maid.

Unknown to Natalie, math teacher Bruce Tucker observed her with interest from her first day on the faculty. Bruce, age forty, had lost his wife in an accident three years before, and was now over the shock enough to begin to look for new pastures. When it was Speedy Johns' turn to host the Friday night coaches' party, Bruce asked him to invite Natalie.

Speedy was glad to hear Bruce say he was interested in a woman. "Am I hearing you right, Bruce? You really want me to ask a female to come to the party? Boy, I'd decided you were going to be celibate." At Coach Johns' remarks, both he and the lanky assistant track coach laughed. "Natalie Shires, hey, that's not a bad idea. So you're finally coming back into the real world!" Speedy had a great respect for his assistant. Bruce was a demanding math teacher, a knowledgeable field events coach, and his best friend.

Natalie saw Bruce walk toward her, carrying a plate of food, and pushing his glasses up on his nose. "Hi there, Miss Natalie Shires, mind if I sit down?" As Bruce said it, he stood above her, waiting for a reply before he seated himself.

Natalie laughed a soft, musical sound which appealed to Bruce. "I'd be delighted if you'd sit down, but I didn't know we were being so formal. Your good manners are showing."

"Good, I'm glad I could catch you alone. I've been wanting to talk to you, but with our busy schedules, and trying to take care of my kids, there's not much time to get together at school. Tell me about yourself. You know you're a bit of a mystery."

Again Natalie laughed. "I'm about as much a mystery as an open-faced sandwich. I moved here from Toledo, Ohio and went to school at Bowling Green University near Toledo. I live with my mother at the Lake Honey Mobile Home Park. Now I've told you the whole deep mysterious side of my life." They both laughed at the simplistic explanation, more at ease than either had anticipated.

Natalie had been busy with her beginning school duties. Lesson plans, school disciplinary procedures, students' names, all these had taken her time and the past few weeks had passed in a blur of activity. She knew most of the teachers' names but knew very little about them. She now looked at Bruce Tucker, thinking how sad he looked and her naturally soft heart melted just a little. "Now that you know my dark secrets, tell me about yourself. Is your wife here with you?" She saw a shadow pass across his face and realized she might have said the wrong thing.

"My wife was killed in an automobile accident three years ago."

"Oh, I'm so sorry!" Natalie blushed as she spoke.

"You wouldn't have any way of knowing, and it's okay. It never gets easy but I've become used to the idea. It happened after a football game almost exactly three years back. I was off scouting a ball game with one of the other coaches and she and my two kids were going home from the game. It had started raining, and you know how the visibility is on these tarmac roads. Some trucker had pulled a flatbed truck over to the side of the road, left it unmarked with no lights on, and didn't get it all the way off the road. The truck was dirty and almost invisible, she never saw it, and hit it without ever knowing it was there. Both the children came out of it unhurt but she died instantly. We had lived a life of quiet contentment and it's been hard to get used to." There was a catch in his throat. "Forgive me, I don't mean to be maudlin, but the memory is never very far from me."

"How terrible for you, and for the children. How are they?"

"They're really doing better than I thought they would. Not that is hasn't been awful, the whole process of adjustment. You know, people say that when a loved one dies, it becomes easier with time. I guarantee you the first six months it didn't get any easier. I cried every day when I was by myself. There was a song about that time, called 'My Woman, My Wife'. It didn't describe Evelyn, but boy, if that one didn't break me up every time I heard it." Big tears welled up in Natalie's eyes, and she wiped at them with her fingers.

He continued, "The kids are doing fine now. Little Evelyn is seven and Rob is ten. They miss her terribly, and I'm sure you can read the sadness in some of their actions, but they've bounced back and they're really pretty happy children. They're so good. They've been as good at straightening me out as I have helping them. Little Evie, I call her Evie instead of Evelyn, she's naturally a happy kid, and Rob is into little league baseball and football, and takes himself quite seriously." He paused, "Say, we've been so deep into this conversation, we're forgetting to eat."

The buffet was sumptuous. There was sliced turkey, beef, and ham, hot meat dishes, vegetables, relish trays, fruit of all kinds, salads, breads, crackers, chips, and dips, desserts, soft drinks, beer, and wine. There was far more than they could possibly eat and it was the most light-hearted time of the week for all.

Natalie and Bruce sat in the large living room, their

heaped plates on their laps, candlelight throwing flickering shadows across their relaxed faces. "Where are you from, Bruce? You don't have a southern accent any more than I." Natalie took a sip of the warming sweet white wine.

Bruce said, "You know, we're all Yankees to the people in the South. I grew up in Michigan and went to Western Michigan when I got out of the service. I was a pole vaulter at Western, and it was there I met Evelyn. I was in Florida part of the time in the Air Force, and I came back here when I finished college. I've been here twelve years and both children were born here."

Natalie put her plate on a nearby coffee table and clasped her hands in front of one knee. "I know you're head of the math department. What do you teach?"

"Like most long time heads of departments, I get to teach the subjects I like best. I have second year algebra and advanced math. Some years I teach geometry, it depends on the demand."

She said, "I know what you mean about teaching the subjects you like best. I'm low woman on the totem pole, so I'm teaching a lot of what no one else wants. I have two classes in remedial English and two in world history. At least they gave me one class in college prep American Government. That must have been to keep me from running back to Ohio." They both laughed at her statement. "You know the last one hired gets the hardest jobs."

Sounds from the kitchen penetrated the other rooms of the open-style house. The lighthearted voices of the wives who were used to each other's company, the more strident voices of the coaches who were intent on the scores being flashed on the television, these put movement into the evening.

Principal Oscar Seidthorn had a talent for being pompous. In conversation with his long-suffering secretary, he was expounding on school discipline. Beth Hagman had the spellbound attention of her date, a preppy looking elementary school physical education instructor.

Bruce Tucker, also an admirer of Beth's charm, winked at Natalie and nodded toward Beth and her mesmerized date. Natalie took in the situation and a smile of understanding flicked across her face. Also in the room were two of the retired coaches who had put in many years at Citrus City High School and were usually included in all things associated with the school athletic program.

Natalie, only now beginning to recognize some of the local citizens who were deeply interested in the school programs, looked at the older men. They had wrinkles, bald spots, gray hair, all merit badges earned in the search of victories, late night bus trips, sandwich meals made necessary by an always limited budget. These men had great interest in athletes who sometimes admired them and at other times only tolerated them. There was still some evidence of the powerful physiques and athletic prowess of the retired coaches. Now their interests were golf and manicuring the lawn. Natalie thought it was a most wonderful change for her, a chance to become part of a school, a community, a new way of life.

Bruce began a conversation with Blackie Warren who had come into the room and was standing, eating a big brownie with ice cream. Natalie had time to study the math teacher who had made her evening so enjoyable. She knew he was older than she was because of all he had done. Still he looked young, sad but young.

Natalie was not one to brood over her unmarried condition. Her father's death, her mother's need for her support, the pressure of teaching school, all these had made the years flow so fast that Natalie did not consider herself an old maid. She just wasn't married yet. It surely was nice not to be in Miss Pemberton's School.

She looked at Bruce, wondering if he was the right man for her. He was tall and she liked that. Still had most of his hair. Bruce had a deep voice, deep but quiet, sort of soothing. Be careful, Natalie, you may make him into something he is not.

Bruce and Blackie were in a light conversation, each smiling and at ease. Natalie had heard enough about Coach Warren's wife to know that if she liked someone, they must have some good qualities, and she seemed to like Bruce.

Blackie drifted away and he turned back to Natalie. "What d'you say we find ourselves some dessert."

"That sounds wonderful. I thought I might help Mrs. Warren eat part of hers, it looked so good." Bruce followed Natalie into the Florida room to the buffet. There was so much that it looked as though it had barely been touched. He looked over the desserts, picked out a slab of cherry pie, and watched as Natalie duplicated Blackie's ice cream and brownie dessert. Then they retreated to the farthest corner of the living room, away from the din.

Natalie wondered if Bruce felt that he was being unfair to his dead wife, but she was glad he seemed content to be with her. She wondered if he'd had a date in the three years since the accident.

Bruce's glasses kept slipping down his nose. He pushed them up and asked, "What kind of music do you like?"

"Oh, I like the 50's and 60's music, light and sweet and slow. I don't like the classics unless they have pretty melodies or wonderful orchestration, and I'm not much into rock music. Gershwin, Rogers and Hammerstein, people like that please me."

"How'd you like to go to a good pops piano concert with

me tomorrow night?"

"Oh, Mister Tucker, I'd love it." Natalie was thrilled. With dates few and far between, her sudden thrust into some social life, this interesting man, a chance to go hear some music she'd really enjoy, it was all exciting.

"Well, let me put it this way, if you call me Mister Tucker one more time, the date's off. My name is Bruce. I like the semi-classics, so we should both enjoy the music."

She said, "I thought the Beatles were outstanding composers, though I don't admire them. I love what the kids call dental office music and I like a good sound system though I'd like to keep my hearing so I don't like it when the amplifiers blow you out of a room. I don't mean to give you a lecture on music, but I play piano and I've been exposed to all kinds."

Bruce said, "I'm glad you're going with me. I'll pick you up about 5:30 and we can have a leisurely dinner in Lakeland. The concert's at eight. Now, I hope you'll excuse me, I'd better go. My children are at my neighbor's house and I don't want to leave them there too long." A faraway look came into his eyes as he said, "They depend on me so much."

"Natalie, getting acquainted with you is the nicest thing that's happened to me for a long time. You'd better tell me where you live."

They both laughed when Natalie said, "It might be easier for you to pick me up if you know my address. Do you know where Lake Honey Mobile Home Park is?"

"Sure, some of our teachers live there."

"Okay, we're at one fifteen Mockingbird Lane. When you pass the gate, take the third street on the right, it's the third home on the right. A math teacher ought to be able to figure that out." They both laughed again, then Bruce left to pick up his children.

# 15

# THE CONCERT

NATALIE'S MOTHER WAS NOT AS THRILLED about the young woman's date as Natalie was. In fact she was madder than hell. If someone had told Amanda Shires she was jealously guarding her daughter from men, selfishly keeping her from being married, she would have said, "Rubbish!" However, no man was ever good enough, stable enough, or from an adequate background. Some unspoken words were, "My offspring, you'll never get married as long as I can help it." Amanda told her, "If I had known that after bringing you to Florida, you'd throw yourself at the first available man, we'd have stayed in Toledo."

"But Mother, I haven't thrown myself at this man, he's just a pleasant faculty member who's asked me to go to a concert with him." She didn't dare tell her mother how much she'd thought about Bruce since the night before.

The two women sat at the white formica-topped breakfast table, looking out over the ixora hedge to the healthy orange grove beyond. The October sun was kinder than it had been in August, but air conditioning was needed this morning.

Amanda had a marvelous idea. "Why don't you just call and tell him I'm ill and you need to stay with me?"

"But Mother, you're not ill and you taught me very young that I shouldn't lie. You play bridge and join in all the park activities. I'm not a child and I have a right to my own life and I'm going with Bruce Tucker to the concert. I'm sorry if it makes you unhappy, but I'm going."

When Bruce arrived, he expected to meet Natalie's mother, but she had taken to her bed and didn't make an appearance.

"Is your mother ill?" Bruce seemed genuinely concerned.

A rather grim look crossed Natalie's usually placid face. "I think it's just a migraine. She'll be all right by morning."

They went to a seafood restaurant perched beside a large lake. They sat on an enclosed porch overlooking the water. People were being unloaded from a glistening streamlined boat onto the pier which was attached to the restaurant. It was all very different for Natalie. To be out of the northern city and in the semi-tropical atmosphere of central Florida, to be involved in the intense football mood of a public high school, to be out on a date with a man who was genuinely attractive to her, all seemed too good to be true.

She thought how difficult it was to deal with her mother. She knew if she dated Bruce or any other man consistently, it would be a battle all the way as it had always been. Amanda felt threatened by Bruce Tucker. Natalie knew what was in her mother's mind, though she wouldn't have said it. Natalie was her meal ticket, her good life. The combination of Natalie's paycheck and Mrs. Shires' social security check made life pleasant, though not plush. If some man came along and took Natalie away from her, Amanda could not live at the same standard she had become used to. She would have to scrape along on her limited savings and her social security check. She might even have to get food stamps. The thought was appalling to the older woman and Natalie knew her mother would try to see that it didn't happen.

Bruce's voice brought Natalie's thoughts back to the table. "I hope you like seafood, it's really good here."

"What are you going to have?"

"I nearly always have the fisherman's platter. If you eat that, you can find what you like best."

She knew if she ordered what he did, she wouldn't make him spend too much.

The skinny waitress with the restaurant logo on her shirt, the obvious tourist families, the extremely informal dress, each facet was interesting to Natalie.

Bruce was easy to be with. Apparently curious about how she was accepting the intense football mood at the high school, he asked, "Tell me, what d'you think of all the excitement over the football season?"

"I've never seen anything like it. You know I've been in a rather exclusive girls' school, hidden away from the public schools. It was almost like a convent and this is so much different, some ways better and some ways worse. We had more control over the students and fewer discipline problems. Citrus City's preoccupation with the football team is disturbing. It's as if winning the state championship was the most important thing in the world. The players are so big and muscular and mature it's almost scary. And that Streets Jackson, he frightens me."

Bruce laughed. "He frightens a lot of people. Some of them are our opponents, and we're glad of that. You know, he's a marvelous athlete and is very bright, but he has a problem. He has a huge chip on his shoulder, always daring anyone to knock it off. His father was killed when he was a young boy and the family's always had hard going. He takes it personally, is continually striking out at the world, trying to get even. We're scared it'll get out of hand." He paused and said, "What do you think of Coach Warren?"

"Oh! He's scrumptious! He's so handsome, and a gentleman, too. It surprises me, I thought all football coaches were dumb and I find he knows more about English than I do. I thought coaches just coached, I didn't know they taught classes."

"You've been sheltered, Natalie. Are you sure that place you taught wasn't a convent?" They both were amused. "Seriously, you know it takes billions of dollars to run the schools, and that money has to be spread over so many things that coaches are primarily teachers and only receive a supplement for coaching. That supplement isn't usually very large. If they don't coach for the love of it and the prestige which sometimes goes with it, they're in the wrong business."

Natalie had a concerned look. "But the winning seems to important. To most of the athletes, the sport is more important than their classes."

"You're right, and we must change that. It's an evil that's crept into the American school system, and it must be driven out somehow. I'm afraid it won't be easy because it's become a part of the American culture. These foreign kids who come into this country, the Asians, are moving to the head of the class, taking the valedictory and salutatory positions away from our native-born students because our Anglo and black kids will not apply themselves to their books to the same degree. The Asians are the ones who are going to the professional schools and will be taking the good jobs while our kids just sit on their fannies. Don't get me started on that or I'll be up on this table preaching to the people." A dark look crossed the face of the math teacher.

By the time they finished the meal, Natalie felt pleasantly full and delighted with the conversation. There was more to this relaxed, interesting man than she had realized. There was an innate goodness, an undercurrent of good humor, the right amount of seriousness.

The piano concert was in the new entertainment auditorium of the community college. Each seat had a good view and the acoustics were excellent. The pianist presented a program of light classics and pops. Natalie was delighted with the selection.

On the way home she told Bruce, "I'm so glad there's good entertainment near Citrus City. There were so many cultural advantages to be gained by living in Toledo, I was afraid that when we moved here, we might be coming to the raw frontier."

He was amused at her perception of Florida. "Don't worry, honey, you're not too far out in the sticks. When Disney moved near here, a thousand good musicians moved to the area, and with the increase in the number of colleges, you can be entertained as much as you want."

When the couple turned into the drive of the spacious mobile home park, Bruce took Natalie's hand. "I want you to know I've enjoyed this evening very much. You're easy to talk to, and I want to see more of you."

Natalie was thrilled. "I've loved every minute of it. It's the nicest thing that's happened to me since I've been here."

He squeezed her hand and released it. They turned off the divided drive on Mockingbird Lane into the concrete driveway. As they did, a light in the back of the mobile home went out. Perhaps Amanda Shires wasn't too sick.

Natalie didn't try to talk to her mother. It had been too nice an evening and she didn't want to spoil it.

# 16

# Angus Talks to Streets

I had a planning period during the third hour, from ten to eleven o'clock. On Monday following the party, I called the office. "Good morning, Ginny, how are things at headquarters?"

"Hi Angus. We're fine up here. How's the Bear Bryant of the high school ranks?" The cheerful redhead got along well with most everyone.

"I'm fine, Ginny. I need to see Streets Jackson if you can get him for me. He's in Bruce Tucker's algebra class so how about getting on the intercom and sending him down to me?"

"Okay, Greek God, you know I will." She liked me because I asked for no undue privileges.

On the intercom, Ginny called Mr. Tucker's class. "Mr. Tucker?"

"This is Bruce Tucker, how may I serve you?" The class giggled, easily distracted by the conversation.

"Coach Warren needs to see Streets Jackson down at the gym. If he's not taking a test, please send him down there."

"He's on his way." The students seldom objected to being called out of class.

"Thank you, and please excuse the interruption." The intercom clicked off.

Streets' unsmiling face appeared in the steel framed doorway of my tiny office. Jackson was not given to light-heartedness and I knew that, but the seriousness on his face was startling. There were dark waters flowing inside that head.

"Hello Streets, how're you doin'?"

"Okay, Coach, what d'you want me for?"

"I need to have a talk with you, Streets. First, let me tell you that you have been playing good football. You've got the state sportswriters and college scouts watching."

"Thanks, Coach," a fleeting smile appeared on the face of the intense young man. "Now, what d'you want to talk about?"

I could see no small talk here, no easy way to say what needed to be said to make the football season roll along smoothly. Here was a star athlete with home problems and ego problems, who needed to be handled carefully for his own sake and for the team.

"Streets, you're smart enough to know that it's hard to coach a team so that the season goes without any problems...."

He interrupted, "What's all that got to do with me?"

"Well, you're probably the best football player we've got,

but you don't have much patience with the other players when they make a mistake that affects you."

"I don't see why I should have. I don't mess up and make them look bad like they do me." Jackson stood in front of my old desk, arms folded across his muscular chest, his thighs bulging against his neat, faded jeans. Streets was angry at me and I could see he felt I had no right to talk to him like this after he had won so many ball games for us.

"Streets, I'm not trying to aggravate you. I'm proud to have you on my football team; I know how valuable you are to Citrus City. I just wish you'd realize there are other good football players out there with you and that part of your success is due to them." I expected some kind of positive answer and got none. I decided that the talk was going nowhere and changed the subject. "How's your mother?" I knew most of the players' parents and was interested in them, so this wasn't idle chatter.

He shrugged his shoulders. "She's okay, Coach. She's got arthritis but she keeps movin'. It don't go away so I guess she's got to live with it." Jackson relaxed a little and I was sure he hoped he wouldn't get fussed at about his huge show of temper in the Dover game.

I tried to put the athlete at ease. "You know what Satchel Paige said, "Keep movin' and don't look back cause somethin' might be gainin' on you."

Jackson laughed a little and I realized I never saw him completely relaxed and happy. I'd never heard a belly laugh from Streets.

He asked, "Can I go back to class now?"

"Sure, Streets, and thanks for coming down." It was a most disappointing conference and I felt I had accomplished absolutely nothing. I decided I wouldn't become a clinical psychologist.

# 17

# Streets Takes a Walk

Coach Caleb Johnson's bass voice boomed above the smacking of the shoulder pads and helmets, above the grunt of the big, talented football players charging into one another.

I stood by the line coach, watching his intense players working on techniques. They were good because they were talented and knew what they were doing; were well coached and physically mature.

Five games and still undefeated. I thanked God for that, though I didn't think God cared who won a football game. We had not incurred any serious injuries and none of the first team had any eligibility problems. I thought, "Heavy, heavy hangs over your head." I hoped the good fortune held but knew the percentages were not in our favor that we should go through a season with no major problems. Everything had to go right to win them all.

Watching Caleb Johnson work with the linemen was like watching an artist at work. He had come from one of the great football programs of the nation, Grambling University. Well trained himself, Coach Johnson had a deep love for all people and his healthy affection for his players was returned with interest. He could have been a line coach at any university.

I caught him away from the scrimmage for a moment. "How's it goin', Caleb?"

"Fine, Angus. The injuries to the linemen aren't too bad. Larson's still limping on his sprained ankle, and Green got his hand stepped on. He's havin' it x-rayed, but I don't think any bones are broken. I've gone over Weirton's strengths and weaknesses in the line." He paused and asked, "Did the extra films on Weirton come in?" These films were very important to us since we could sometimes find opponents' weaknesses or see a strategic advantage from studying the films.

"No, Coach. We may have to get along without 'em."

I decided I was interfering with Coach Johnson's line practice so I went to make sure the kicking practice was going well. They were slow getting the kicks off in the last two games and I needed to speed them up because it might make the difference in winning or losing a game.

I watched the two extra point and field goal kickers for ten minutes. They worked kicking both from the center and from the hash marks. We had missed several extra points and the kickers needed to improve.

Callahan was practicing pass patterns with his receivers, and Speedy Johns was giving special attention to the sideline passes. Callahan ran the passes over and over, throwing many times to each receiver.

Standing by the kickers, I heard Streets Jackson's strident voice raised in the area where the ends and backs were practicing. Streets was screaming at one of the other backs, yelling curses that would curl your hair. We had a team rule against cursing. My staff did not swear and I did not allow the players to swear. What they did away from school I couldn't control and I knew some of them cursed when they were out of my hearing. I started toward the area where the backs and ends were practicing, where Streets was screaming at the other player.

"Hell no, that's no way to run that pattern!" There was no mistaking Streets' voice. He was berating one of the second string players who was defending himself.

"But that's what the play book—"

"I don't give a damn what the play book shows, that's not the way you run that route!"

I jogged over to where the two players were having their confrontation. By this time, all the backs and ends had stopped practicing and were watching the argument. Where Streets was involved, anything could happen. Coach Johns had gone to the dressing room to answer a phone call, so he wasn't here to settle the problem.

I felt the situation had gone so far that I had no choice but to make a point. "Knock it off, Streets, you know the rule on cursing, and if you can't follow the same rules as everyone else, you'd better take the day off."

Jackson's mouth fell open. It was preposterous because you didn't talk that way to the star athlete, even if you were the head coach. "You can't send me home, honky, 'cause you need me. I am your football team."

I did not mean for the situation to reach this critical point. It had blown up so suddenly and now I knew the point of no return had been passed. Reluctantly, I said, "Okay, Jackson, we'll see if we can make it without you. Go turn in your uniform." It was some of the hardest words I had ever uttered.

Streets was furious. "You sendin' me home? Honky, you'll lose without me. Watch what I say, you'll lose without me." As he said it he pointed his finger at me. With that, the multitalented athlete stalked off the field toward the dressing room, swaggering as he went, coming up high on one foot and then the other. His shoulders moved from side to side as he walked, his gait controlled by his emotions.

I was numb the rest of the day. Until the outburst happened, I hadn't noticed the gray scud clouds which had blown in from the northwest, casting a pall over us. The practice was flat and there was a hush over the team as the best football player in the state had just been sent home. The team's every waking thought was of the football season and the state championship. They could hear footsteps. Everything we had all worked for for years was in imminent danger of falling apart.

When I was in bed that night, I cried for the first time in many years.

# 18

# Game Seven Sharpton

THE FIFTY-FIVE PLAYER SHARPTON HIGH School team burst onto the stadium turf, running full speed, looking more like a college team than high school players. Sharpton's football team was a sleeping giant which had come to life. They looked powerful, aggressive, and confident.

This was the seventh game of the season and we had lost Streets from the team. Nobody could fill his shoes, and true to what the dynamic rebel had said, we had lost a game. Now we were in a three-way tie for the district lead with Weirton and with this Sharpton team that was improving every week.

Sharpton had started the season as an unknown quantity. They had been third in the eight-team district the previous year, had lost several players through graduation, and had struggled through the first four games of the season. Glades View had knocked them off in the season opener, then they bounced back to win the next three by narrow margins. In the fifth game, Sharpton's running and passing suddenly blossomed and they steamrolled a big Orlando school, 40 to 14.

After the sixth game, at the coaches' party, we had been unwinding from the emotional, heart-wrenching action of the losing football game. As we watched the Tampa TV station roll the scores of the area games, Sharpton's 40 to 14 victory came on the screen.

"Great Lord have mercy," I said. "Fellahs, as if we didn't already have enough trouble, would you look at that score!"

Sharpton had improved every week and their victory over the Orlando School was no fluke. The following week they won by more than fifty points. We had a week off, but now it was our turn to deal with them.

The big, colorful, talented bands blared their music across the field, taunting each other with the sound. Cheerleaders bounced through their primitive ceremony, drawing response from several thousand pairs of vocal cords. Our two teams had been waiting at the ends of the field and they ran through the paper barriers being held by the frenetic pep squad members and lined up in front of the wooden benches on opposite sides. The team captains met in the center of the field for the toss of the coin. We won the toss and our co-captains King and Michler chose to receive. We took the opening kickoff and battered our way for a touchdown. I thought to myself, "So far, so good."

In the first quarter, the veteran Michler got up slowly from a pile-up of players and hobbled off the field. I could see dark clouds gathering because now I was playing without my number one back and my best lineman.

On the kickoff following our touchdown, they gave us a dose of our own medicine. Sharpton's right side deep back caught the ball, then started left and handed off to the other deep back running right. Our outside defender was cut down with a staggering block and a wall was formed down the right side of the field and the runner scored untouched. The Sharpton fans roared their approval and their band shook the stands with their victory song.

With the changing tone of the game, I broke into a cold sweat. Following the Sharpton touchdown and extra point, their kicker booted the football to our five where sure-handed Marty Oliver took it on the run and headed straight upfield behind a vee of blockers. At the twenty, a frenzied Sharpton player put his helmet into the ball, and the ball flew high into the air where another Sharpton player pulled it into his arms, bounced hard against one of our players and twisted away from him. The alert ball carrier instantly saw the flow of players was to the right so he cut left against the grain and burst into the open. He covered the remaining fifteen yards like a gazelle. As he scored, pandemonium broke loose in the Sharpton stands and their band blared louder than ever. There was a hush on our side of the field as we tried to figure out what had happened to our powerhouse. Both teams had been successful on extra point attempts. In less than seven minutes, the score was Sharpton 14, Citrus City 7.

My coaching staff was shell-shocked. Coach Johnson studied his clipboard, looking for an idea. I was standing next to him and he said, "It looks like another bad Friday, Angus. D'you want to make some changes?"

"Well, Caleb, I know it looks bad but I don't think we need to panic. All year long we've been doing things right, let's don't make any big changes if we don't have to."

It wasn't our night. On our next possession, the

unpredictable happened when Callahan stepped away from the center too fast and the ball squirted loose. The charging Sharpton nose man fell on the ball in plain view of our stands as eight thousand frustrated fans groaned in unison.

The Sharpton coaches took advantage of Michler's absence and drove play after play over his substitute. Since Streets was missing from the defensive backfield, I switched Hunky King into the linebacker spot behind Michler's substitute, then we stopped them. On the fourth down, with eight yards needed, they lined up to kick a field goal. There was quiet from the stands as the ball was centered to the holder. The Sharpton kicker drove the ball hard but low at the crossbar. It hit the crossbar, went straight up, hit the bar again and bounced over for the score. Their fans went wild...Again.

We went into the dressing room at halftime with the scoreboard reading Sharpton 17, Citrus City 7. As we tramped our cleats across the cement leading into the dressing room, I looked among the fans to see the grinning face of Streets Jackson and I felt deeply the silent laugh of the rebellious athlete.

Halftime was deadly quiet. While our trainer worked on Michler's swollen ankle, I talked to the other coaches. We weren't used to being behind and I asked Speedy if he had any ideas.

"Sure, Angus, but first we've got to remember that both their touchdowns were flukes, things that shouldn't happen to a team as good as we are. They're the best we've faced all year and we can't get caught with another touchdown on the kickoff or on punts, so we've got to go back to our three-man backup system. That's number one. The backs have gotta hold the ball like they never held it before because we sure can't stand any fumbles."

I nodded agreement, then turned to the rock, Caleb Johnson, who was such a steadying influence. The coach, pausing to answer a player's question, grinned when he turned to me. "It's a tough ball game, Angus, so don't get your bowels in an uproar. The ball's bounced right for Sharpton three times but we'll come back, mark my word. Let's keep on with our game plan. We've got Hunky where we need him, and without Jackson, we're not as explosive, but we're still the best team on the field. I say, let's take it to 'em."

I couldn't see that getting emotional would do any good. I let the players rest most of the fifteen minutes and then told them, "Okay, fellahs. We're behind in this ball game and we're not used to it and we don't like it. All you ball carriers look at me. When you've got the ball, hold on to it and squeeze like you've never squeezed before. Quarterbacks, when you take the ball from the center, move up into the snap before you back away. You guys know these things, just don't forget them. Sharpton's good but we're better so now let's go out and win a ball game."

The intensity on the faces of the players, the worried looks of the coaches, each pointed to the importance we gave this sport of football. It's true, many of these players felt that football was more important than school subjects or grades, and it's easy for the coaches to put it number one in our lives. Right now, it seemed terribly important.

We kicked off to Sharpton to open the second half. Marty Oliver did the kicking for us and the kick was a towering end over end boot that went over the head of the Sharpton receiver and out of the end zone. Our fans screamed their approval. From their twenty, Sharpton ran a play over Larson for a gain of three. In the Sharpton huddle, the quarterback must have decided to take advantage of

Michler's absence. We shifted our defense to confuse them as the quarterback barked the signals in a high-pitched voice. At the count of two, Sharpton's linemen surged forward, the quarterback handed the ball to his fullback who rammed the right tackle spot. The linemen double-teamed our defensive end and the fullback burst through the line of scrimmage just in time to be bombed by Hunky King. King hit the ball carrier at full speed and the collision could be heard at the farthest corner of the stadium. The Sharpton ball carrier lay writhing on the damp grass, trying to get his breath.

King bent over the big fullback, "You all right, man?" Pain showed in the fullback's eyes, but he nodded to Hunky. The Sharpton coach and trainer helped the player to his feet and the three walked to the sidelines together. On both sides of the field, the spectators applauded to show they were glad that the athlete's injury was not serious.

If the modern world has a parallel to the Roman Coliseum and the gladiators, this is it. The colorful, noisy crowds, even the violence lent some of the same flavor.

Sharpton ran one more play and was forced to punt. The spiraling ball came down on our thirty-eight where Marty gathered it in and drove it back to midfield.

On our first offensive play, I had Callahan call for the screen pass. When he faded back, the line check-blocked the Sharpton defensive line, then let them through. The eager, hard-charging defenders took the bait and surged at Callahan. Buck flipped the ball into the waiting arms of Benny Wells and he was eleven yards downfield before he was knocked out of bounds. That gave us a first and ten at the Sharpton thirty-nine. Buck ran the option right, a big hole opened for the fullback and with precision the quarterback palmed the ball against Johnny Blocker's belt buckle. The play went for fourteen yards before a defensive halfback grabbed Blocker's jersey and wrestled him to the ground. With the ball at the twenty-five, the Sharpton safety man was playing out of position, farther to his left than normal, so I sent in a halfback pass to our left end. Callahan faked the handoff to Blocker and as a defensive lineman loomed before Buck, he lateraled to Oliver. Left end Tatum had delayed to let the flow of the teams go with the option play right, then he broke over the center with the flow and cut sharply back to the area left deserted by the safety man. Oliver's pass hit Tatum on the Sharpton five and he scored with no one near him.

Our frustrated fans jumped to their feet and the band broke into the school song. The extra point was good and the score now read: Sharpton 17, Citrus City 14.

The two teams battled back and forth through the third quarter and halfway through the fourth with Sharpton still three points ahead. I was so worried that I had taken my cap off and put it on a hundred times. With four minutes to go, Sharpton drove to our thirty-four, mixing their passing and running game with unrelenting efficiency. With third and six, the elusive Sharpton quarterback dropped back into the pocket, and drew back his arm just as the flanker broke into the clear near the goal line. I could see the whole picture as if it were in slow motion and I cringed as the rifle arm came forward. At that instant our nose guard Porter Green blasted his way past the defending linemen, hitting the quarterback as he released the ball, deflecting it upward on a wobbly, shortened path. Hunky King raced under the hanging ball, gathered it into his arms on the run, broke past the Sharpton team and covered the sixty-six yards to the goal line with flashing speed. Our kicker missed the extra point but it was all over.

Michler went back into the game and we shut down their potent offense. The game ended twenty to seventeen and we were still in the race for the state championship. The Sharpton coach was so discouraged he would not shake my hand after the game but I understood. He had a right to be frustrated after his team had played so well and lost.

# 19

# Gertrude Jackson

Gertrude Jackson's legs ached. The tall, rawboned woman stood in the sectionizing line of the drafty Golden Hill citrus plant, picking up the blistering hot grapefruit. She deftly removed the skin which was heated to make the peeling come off easily, then cut out the succulent sections with amazing quickness. The engorged varicose veins on Gertrude's tired legs throbbed with constant pain.

It was Friday night and Streets would be at the ball game before she left the plant. He wasn't playing because he had been kicked off the team, but Gertrude knew he couldn't stay away from the game. Streets hadn't told her about his expulsion but the neighbors sure had.

"How come Streets been put off the football team, Gertrude?" May Ann, who drove the car taking Gertrude and three other sectionizers home from work, couldn't wait to dig at Gertrude with the question.

"Yeah, I heard that temper of his done got him in trouble with the coach." Another voice heard from.

Gertrude didn't explode. With calm resignation, learned from ten thousand of her children's crises, she spoke to no one in particular. "That boy worries me more'n all the others put together. He's the smartest but he feels things the mos'. He still blames the world because my husban' Henry ran into that freight train." She laughed a nonhumorous laugh. "Streets could go to college an' really be somebody if he don' mess up on the way. I haven't had time to talk to Caleb Johnson about him gettin' kicked off the team but I know he'll tell it like it is."

Darkness had settled and a light rain was falling, and as they drove home from work they talked about the team. Three of the women in the car had sons playing on the team and they were intensely interested in the conversation. Too interested. All were tired from standing on their feet for eleven hours in the drafty sectionizing plant. They didn't see the mottled pickup truck with the inexperienced immigrant driver pull out of the parking lot of a dimly lit bar. The parking lot was small and partly hidden from view by an eight foot wooden fence. The pickup driver, anesthetized from four welcome beers, didn't realize his lights were not on when he pulled out of the beer joint into the path of May Ann's dark green Dodge. Too late, May Ann jammed on her brakes and pulled left in an attempt to avoid the collision, but when they banged into the pickup, all five women were thrown violently forward and to the right. Gertrude was in the right rear seat and catapulted against the window, cracking it with her head, then instantaneously slid forward against the window frame and doorpost. She was slammed into unconsciousness.

Amid the confusion of whirling red and blue lights, the white-coated emergency medical technicians worked efficiently, placing the women and the confused Mexican into the waiting ambulances. Two city police cruisers and one county deputy kept the crowd from getting in the way. As the stocky technician bent over Gertrude, he whispered to his helper, "This one don't look too good to me. She is plumb out of it, so we better be mighty careful movin' her."

The women in the accident with Gertrude were examined, then dismissed from the cold white emergency room and the driver of the pickup truck was declared fit to make a trip to the police station. When Gertrude was moved to intensive care, the veteran trauma physician on duty spoke to the nurse in charge, "This patient isn't responding at all and with that bump on her head, she may be unconscious for a while. I can't find any broken bones, but that would be the least of her problems. That's Streets Jackson's mother and she had eight kids at home, so I sure hope she comes out of this all right."

At the football field, Streets leaned his taut body against the four foot chain link fence which separated the composition track from the football field. True to his prediction, the Spartans were behind before the first quarter was over. Few people spoke to the fierce athlete. Only the large men and the pretty women dared because it was better to say nothing to Streets than to say the wrong thing.

When halftime came, with the Spartans trailing in the ball game, he purposely hung around the area where the team and coaches had to pass on the way to the dressing room. As the sweaty, dirt-encrusted players passed by Streets, he grinned at them. They were confused by the score and Jackson's attitude. He wanted them to lose! When Streets caught the coaches' eyes, a big malicious smile darted across his face.

At the beginning of the second half, the crowd could hear sirens and the sound seemed to be coming from north of town. There were too many sirens for the usual accident, most of the spectators figured it must be a fire. Streets heard it and ignored it, because if it didn't concern him, he wasn't interested. At the beginning of the fourth quarter, the public address system blared forth an unusual announcement. "Streets Jackson is wanted at the player's bench. I repeat, will Streets Jackson please report to the player's bench. I repeat, will Streets Jackson please report to the player's bench."

A ripple of approval sounded from the grandstands as the public wanted their high scoring running back in the game. Jackson laughed to himself, thinking, "I guess that big honky Coach Angus Warren found out he can't win without me and he wants me to dress out. He can rot in hell for what he did to me 'cause I'm gonna let him lose this one. Then I can get some satisfaction listening to him beg." Streets sauntered the fifty yards to where the red-and-white-suited second and third team players and the coaches were standing by the sidelines. He looked for Coach Warren, expecting to see him waiting hopefully for his star athlete to come to the rescue. Instead it was Coach Johnson who approached Streets as he walked up. The other players ignored him and that bothered the egotistical Streets.

Caleb didn't wait for Streets to speak. "Son, your mother's been in a car wreck and they need you at the hospital. You get on down there and I'll check with you after the game."

Jackson was stunned. He could count on his mother because she was always there. He ran along the sidelines to the north end of the field, vaulted the short fence, and ran to the gate. He pushed the milling crowd aside as his mind raced, considering the possibilities about his mother's condition. "Oh God, Oh Lord, don't let her die!" Streets raced up the busy avenue toward the hospital which was a half mile away. He covered the distance as fast as it had ever been done on foot. Streets knew the system for getting in the hospital after hours, so he went directly to the brightly lit entrance marked in big red letters, EMERGENCY ENTRANCE, and in smaller letters a sign next to the bell which said, Ring Bell for Attendant. Almost at once, a white-clad orderly opened the door and recognized him.

"You mother's in intensive care, Streets. She got a bad bump on the head so you better go up there and ring the bell and maybe they'll let you see her."

"How bad is she?"

"I honestly don't know," the orderly said, "and if I did I'm not allowed to tell you. You'll have to talk to the nurse in charge and maybe she can tell you something."

Streets ran down the gleaming, sterile corridor to the place where the elevator and stairs stood side by side. He ignored the elevator and took the steps three at a time. He paused at the second floor, glanced at the wall where a sign said INTENSIVE CARE UNIT, with an arrow pointing left. He did not stop at the waiting room but hurriedly rang the buzzer outside the ward.

A severe looking nurse appeared at the door. "You must be one of the Jacksons." She didn't know Streets from reading the sports page and she hadn't watched an athletic event for years. She only used the sports page in her canary cage.

"Yes, ma'am. Now can I see my mothah?"

"I can let you in for fifteen minutes, but I must tell you that she's unconscious and we don't know when her condition might change." She hesitated to say either that Gertrude might become conscious or that her condition might worsen, because she looked bad. She walked with

Streets to the steel bed with the sides on it. Intravenous tubing was attached to Gertrude from two bottles above and Streets took in a big breath. "Her blood pressure and breathing are just about normal, and that's a good sign."

"How come she needs that stuff in her arm?" Everything about the place frightened Streets. His mother looked smaller and older than he expected her to, and that frightened him more. He realized he hadn't really taken a good look at his mother in years.

"We have to give her the IV so we can give her any medicine she needs without waking her, and to keep her body fluids normal. You can stay with her for fifteen minutes, then you'll have to go outside and wait with your family." She walked back to the nurses' station and the observation section in the center of the room.

Streets stood quietly beside the deathly still woman, his naturally erect carriage making him seem as if he were standing at attention. He glanced at the observation station and saw that no one was watching. He gently took his mother's hand and spoke very softly to her. "Momma, Momma, it's me, Streets." He drew no response. Tears gathered in his eyes. "Hey, Momma, please wake up, please wake up, Momma." He gently shook her arm. Almost at once a younger nurse appeared at his side.

"You'd better not shake her, Mr. Jackson. It won't help her and it won't make her wake up any faster. When someone's unconscious, there's usually nothing you can do to make them wake up. It just happens."

The normally fierce young man was for once a heartbroken, quiet child. "I jus' feel so helpless. She's my momma and she's all we got and we need her so bad." His husky voice was so intense that the nurse, used to critical situations, had to turn her head aside for a moment while she gathered her composure.

"She's resting fine right now, Mr. Jackson. Your brothers and sisters are in the waiting room and they're worried just like you are. They need you to be strong, so why don't you go out and talk to them."

Streets didn't know what he was going to say to his family. How do you tell your brothers and sisters that your mother is unconscious and might not wake up at all? His feet dragged as he left the intensive care ward. Fourteen anxious eyes turned to him and he walked over to the sitting area. He could tell they had all been crying. He knew that the older boys hadn't cried for two or three years because older boys don't cry.

"How's Momma, Streets? Is she gonna be all right? She is, ain't she, Streets?" Jonathan's voice pleaded for all of them. It was as if hoping would make it so.

"Sure she is, Jonathan, you know Momma's strong. She's asleep right now." He hoped God would forgive him for this white lie. Suddenly he cared what God thought.

"Can we go an' see her, Streets?" The eight-year-old Princess was the youngest, and if there was a pet in the family, she was it.

"No, honey, they'll only let us in for a few minutes each hour, and then only a couple of us. Let's set here and wait. Y'all get a magazine or somethin' and be kinda quiet."

There was no change in Gertrude Jackson's condition and at 2:30 in the morning a weary and subdued Jackson family were driven home by Coach Johnson who had been with them since 11:30, his presence an anchor for the stricken brothers and sisters. Standing at the bedside, Caleb told Streets, "I'm sure she's going to be just fine, son."

The next day brought no change in Gertrude, and the family was so quiet and intense it affected the whole neighborhood. Friends brought in food and there was no playing. Children who normally sat glued to the television never thought to turn it on. Streets became the master of the house and no one dared disobey him.

That morning, Caleb was in his study at the church. As he sat poring over Bible passages for his Sunday sermon, greying at the temples, a large cross dangling from his neck, he looked more like a biblical patriarch than a football coach. He heard a quiet rapping, and inured to interruptions, ambled patiently to see who needed him. Streets, misery showing in every portion of his face, stood at the threshold. "Can I come in and talk t' you, Coach?"

"Sure, Streets. You know I'm always here for you no matter what's on your mind." Caleb surely expected Streets to start talking about his mother. "How's your mother doing this morning, Son?"

"She ain't no better and she ain't no worse from what the doctors say but I don't think they're tellin' me the truth. I had to get outta there for a little while 'cause I felt so helpless. It seems like I can't help her any."

Caleb shifted in his overburdened chair and said, "I've been in dozens of situations like this, son. The doctors often don't know any more than you or me when someone will come out of unconsciousness. You've just got to take heart from the fact that she's no worse, and remember, you've got to be strong for your family."

"I want to talk to you about somethin' else, Coach. How come the team could turn their back on me at the game?"

"Well, I'll tell you, boy, you turned your back on them at practice the other day and you turned your back on all of us. They let you know that you're not as important as you think."

The word boy infuriated Streets and he screamed back at his coach. "What d'ya mean callin' me boy, nobody calls me boy!"

With movements so fast that Streets was powerless to interrupt them, Caleb Johnson picked Jackson up by the waist and slammed him against the wall, holding him there, squirming like a child. "You listen to me, boy. You ain't nothin' but a boy in a man's body, and you're actin' more like a spoiled brat than anyone I've seen in a long time." He lowered Jackson to a chair but held him in a grip from which Streets was powerless to move. "God gave you one of the finest bodies I've ever seen and he gave you a keen mind which you don't even bother to use, and a fine mother and some decent brothers and sisters. You go to a good school and are coached by people who care. You got a chance to go to college and you're about to mess that up. Here's your mother in a precarious condition and you're still worried about yourself. Now, straighten up or nobody'll want to do anything for you. You go home and spend some time thinkin'."

On Sunday afternoon, forty-four hours after she struck her head on the doorpost, Gertrude Jackson awakened. She was somewhat nauseated and had a bad headache, but for her to be conscious was a miracle for her children. They were excited and were so noisy the nurse had to send half of them home. She left it to Streets to decide who went home, and there was no arguing with his decision.

Before Streets went in to see his mother, the doctor had some words of advice. "Son, her condition's still very serious and you must not upset her. Don't try to spend too much time with her because she needs to rest. Her waking up is a wonderful sign but let's not make her tired. She'll have to be in bed a couple of weeks for sure."

On Monday morning, the younger children told Streets that they wanted to go down to the hospital and "stay with Momma" instead of going to school.

Streets' reaction was instantaneous. "Oh no, we ain't gonna have none of that. Ya'll git dressed and git to school. The only way you can help Momma is by goin' to school and doin' what you're s'posed to. If I hear of any one of you layin' out, I'll beat your fanny. You can run by and see Momma for a short few minutes after school, but don't you make her tired."

That afternoon Gertrude Jackson looked wearily at her powerful young son. She could see the tension in his knuckles when he gripped the bedrail.

Now she spoke quietly, tiredness showing in her voice. "You've had a mad on at the world since you were a little boy, ever since your daddy got killed. Son, it was nobody else's fault. You're tryin' to take it out on everyone, and near as I can tell, the coaches are good people. I know they're tryin' to win games, but more'n that, they're really tryin' to make you boys into better people. Now you've gone and got yourself put off the team and you may lose the only chance you'll ever have of makin' a good livin'. You're sure not workin' hard enough at your school work to git you anywhere. If you think us bein' poor and havin' all those chil'ren is somebody else's fault, you'd better think again. The stork didn't bring 'em. Besides that, you're not as important as you think you are. God gave you that body and it's up to you to do somethin' good with it."

That night, Streets lay in the sagging bed, arm over his forehead, unable to close his eyes as so many thoughts were going through his head. He figured his mother was going to get well and he thanked God. He really thanked God, saying the first prayer he had said for years, that she was conscious and able to talk to him. She was out of intensive care and in a regular room, and the doctors said she was much better.

He thought about the football team. Thinking as he had

for years, he still didn't feel he was completely at fault. Not enough to get him kicked off the team. Maybe he didn't win those games by himself, at any rate, he'd never thought of it that way before. He'd have a hard time going through those defensive lines if somebody didn't block and make holes for him, he'd give 'em that.

Man, he hated to apologize to anyone for anything. He thought, Streets Jackson just don't say I'm sorry to no one. It was true, the coaches had never been unfair to him, but they were there to coach and the athletes won the games. Coach Speedy Johns sure as hell didn't win those races for him. Streets winced as he thought the word hell. Cussin' again, he didn't know if he could stop cussin'. He had cussed ever since he was eight years old and cussin' showed you were a man. Well, he didn't have to show anybody anything.

He thought, "I guess I'll have to go back to that honky, Coach Warren and tell him I'd like to be back on the team. I don't know how I can say it but I sure as hell don't want them to win the championship without me." The thought startled him. Could they win the state championship without him? That Powell was a powerful dude, and someone had told Streets that Coach Johns was moving Powell to Streets' position. Streets wondered how they could even think of giving his running back spot to that big ape. Then he considered that maybe it wasn't his position if he wasn't out there.

Streets tossed and turned in the bed so much that the sheets looked like spaghetti. He sweated and threw the blanket off, then got cold and pulled it back up and turned over on his belly. His smallest brother Rafer finally got tired of the movement and got up to get in bed with his other two sleeping brothers. Streets looked over at the alarm clock radio which read 2:30 in the morning. He started sweating again. His muscles rippled as he started thinking of the last game he played in.

He played over every play he had been a part of. He exulted in the long runs, they were his favorites because they showed everyone his great speed, and the roar of the crowd showed how much they liked him. Well, maybe liked him would be the wrong word because people didn't seem to like him very much. That speed and power, that's where the scholarship would come from. Scholarship. He thought, they'd sure better call it athleteship 'cause he was certainly no scholar. Then he thought, I'll do better with my grades and I could even make the teachers proud of me.

At 6:00, Streets got up more tired than when he had gone to bed. He saw everyone off to school, piled the dishes in the sink, and started to school. During the first change of classes, Streets walked into Coach Warren's office, poked his head in the doorway and asked, "Coach, can I talk to you for a minute?"

"Sure, Streets, what's on your mind?" It was an asinine question as it was on the minds of the whole football team and half the town. Word had also reached Orlando and the region's schools.

"Coach, I don't know how to say this, but I may have made a mistake." There, he'd said it and it didn't hurt near as bad as he thought it would.

There was a moment of silence. "Well now, that might be the understatement of the year, mister Jackson." Streets surely didn't think he was being called mister Jackson out of respect.

"I shouldn't have mouthed off to you like I did, Coach. You know I got a temper and I just let it get away from me. Will you let me back on the football team?"

"It's not that simple, mister Jackson. I don't think it's entirely up to me to let you back on the team. You let me down, you told me I couldn't tell you what to do, you jeopardized your scholarship chances, but a lot more important than that, you let down your team. These are the same guys you've been playing with since you were in little league."

"What d'you mean I jeopardized my scholarship chances?"

"Son," Streets winced at the word son, but he surely didn't think he'd better object to the title. "When an athlete is being considered for a scholarship, the colleges want to know everything about him. They want to know about his grades, his athletic ability, what his family life is like, and how he gets along with other people. They don't need any prima donnas on the football team. It's hard enough for those college coaches to run a program and win when everything is going right for them, so one thing they don't need is an athlete who thinks he's better than other people."

"But I am better than other people, Coach."

"Physically, Streets, you're faster and stronger than most of the athletes we have here, but your attitude stinks. If you do get to go to college on a football scholarship, and right now that's a big if, you'll find that you'll be among the cream of the crop. It won't just be the athletes from one town, but the best from all across the state, many of the best from other states. When you're competing with all those talented athletes, you'll find that many people are just as strong and about as fast as you. Only then will you find out how good your are. Unless you can take orders from me and the other coaches, we don't want you. Somebody has to run the show and that's why the coaches are in charge. If you don't do things our way, you can't play. Even if you wanted to play, it would be up to the team to say it was okay. You'd have to apologize to them."

"Forget it, Coach. Streets Jackson don't apologize to nobody."

"If that's the way it is, Streets, this conversation is over. You'd better get back to class."

# 20

# Game Eight
# Culver

WE DIDN'T HAVE STREETS PLAYING FOR US, BUT when the Citrus City football team gathered in the dressing room before the Culver game, we could feel an electric determination in the air. It was quieter than usual with none of the horseplay and laughter that sometimes preceded a ball game.

First, we gave some serious attention to special plays and specialty team assignments. Then I asked Coach Johnson to talk to the boys before we sent them out on the field. His words were carefully chosen. "You Spartans have a challenge. You're the best big school team in the state of Florida and you've come this far without any serious injuries. Culver is a good football team, so don't take them lightly. I want you to go out there and play football like you've been trained to play, like you've been training since you played little league football years ago. We're superior at running the ball and our passing is better than anybody we've played. We're bigger, stronger, faster, smarter, and better organized than anybody we play. Let's make our blocking and tackling dynamite. Blow Culver out of the way! Let's make this a picture perfect ball game." The big coach clapped his hands and the squad thundered out of the dressing room like a team possessed.

If the Culver High School football coach could have foreseen how his scheduling would put him head to head with Citrus City at this point of the season, he would have avoided it at all costs. He caught the Spartans on the wrong night.

We came out with our full offense, passing and running from the opening kickoff. Powell was in the running back slot where Streets would normally have been, and he tore up and down the field, relentless as a bulldozer. He gained big chunks of yardage, and when the defense pulled in tight to stop Powell, fleet footed Marty Oliver raced around the end. Determined to stop us, Culver's line rushed recklessly at Callahan, only to be suckered by a quick pass, good for a second touchdown with but ten minutes gone in the first quarter.

Early in the second quarter, Culver's quarterback fumbled and an alert Nels Larson was on the ball like a shark on a sting ray. Callahan started picking at the Culver team with short inside passes and with sideline passes. The Culver deep backs edged forward to defend against the short passes and Callahan hit Terry Foote with a post pattern that went for another touchdown. Culver could not move the ball against our steel tight defense. Horst Michler and Marko Parelli spent so much time in the Culver backfield, it seemed they had on the wrong color jerseys.

I figured that somewhere in the stands, Streets was watching the slaughter with great concern for his immediate future. His dreams of fame and of being irreplaceable must be taking a beating about this time. I hoped he was watching the big Powell kid as he knocked tacklers aside with his brute strength and surprising speed.

We kept sending Marty in motion toward the left side of the field with no apparent purpose. He went in motion time after time, until the nearby defender stopped paying any attention to him. In the huddle, Callahan spoke directly to Oliver. "Okay, Marty, if we haven't got the man in motion pass set up, it never will be. Motion pass on two."

If I could have placed every player on the field where I wanted them, it couldn't have been any better. Oliver was five yards behind the defensive back before he knew what was happening, and the ball sailed over the defender's head into Oliver's waiting arms as he crossed the goal line with no one near him.

In the third quarter, with the score thirty-four to nothing, I started substituting the second team into the game. As soon as I saw second-stringers could battle on even terms with Culver, I let them finish the game.

It was a confident, satisfied Citrus City team that trooped off the field, carrying the mantle of victory on their shoulders.

I had tried to keep up with Gertrude Jackson's condition, and I was tremendously relieved to know she was recovering. I wasn't aware of what was going on with Streets and his mother, but I'm sure their conversation would have been a revelation to me.

At the hospital, Streets talked quietly to his mother as she sat up in her bed, looking rested for the first time since she had gone back to work after the summer layoff.

"They did it without me, Momma, and I didn't think

they could. They beat the crap out of Culver, and that Powell boy, he is somethin' else. He was a sorry lineman and now he's a star back. Well, I guess I wouldn't want to be a tackle either."

Gertrude looked up at her powerful son with love in her eyes. "Don't let them winning without you git you down. It don't make you any less than you are; it just maybe taught you a lesson. It only proves you've been playin' with a good team, and now maybe you'll feel like there's somebody out there besides you. You better do whatever you can to git back on that team, you hear?"

# 21

# Streets' Reasoning

When Streets opened the sagging door of his family's house, he had just returned from visiting his mother. She seemed to be recovering, even looked more rested than usual, and Streets was tremendously relieved, even penitent. He thanked God again for letting her become conscious and he was sorry for being a smart ass at football practice. He poured a cup of coffee and sat on the stained couch in the living room, watching television, not paying much attention to the soap operas which he thought were dumb anyhow; the same crap over and over.

For two hours he sat there thinking, greeting his brothers and sisters as they came in but not paying them much attention either. His mind was on the football team as always. After much thought, he again concluded that the blow up at practice had not really been his fault, but he knew if he wanted back on the football team, he'd have to kiss a few asses.

He didn't see how Franklin Powell could run the football as well as he had. In fact, Streets knew Franklin couldn't. The crowds just thought he could because he was so big, and it was mostly a mirage. The more he thought about it, the madder he got and the more Streets knew the football team couldn't get along without him because he was the best there was. He'd show them all a thing or two, he'd just stay away from the coaches and practice for a couple more days, and let them get along without him, and see how they liked that.

Streets sauntered down the middle of town at the same time the football players were coming home from practice. Sauntered was maybe the wrong word, strutted would be a better description. He passed the green convenience store, the beer joint, and the neat gas station, walking on the sidewalk. People stepped aside and nodded to him or avoided him because they didn't want a confrontation. There were plenty around who were not scared of Streets, men who could lift hundred pound boxes of fruit onto the back of a truck all day and weren't scared of anything.

Alfonius Jefferson was a second-string tackle, a good student but not worldly-wise. When he saw Streets, Alfonius grinned and spoke to the volatile athlete. The first words out of his mouth were, "Man, Streets, what'd you think of ol' Franklin Powell? Is he some kind of runnin' back or ain't he." Unwilling to listen to any kind of praise for Powell, Streets did what had earned him his reputation, he hit Alfonius on the point of the chin, decking him. It wasn't a fight because it was so sudden and one-sided.

As Alfonius sat in the Saint Augustine grass, holding his jaw, Streets hollered at him, "I don't want to hear no more about Franklin Powell because he's nobody, he's nothin'!" With that, Streets turned and walked stiffly back home.

The next day, Streets stayed home from school. He visited his mother at the hospital twice, neglecting to tell her about his confrontation with Alfonius because he knew she wouldn't like it. Other than seeing his mother, he sat at home, again watching pointless television.

When Coach Johnson came by and knocked on the door, Streets opened it only a few inches, and in response to the coach's inquiry about his mother, Streets said, "What do you care? Ain't nobody ever cared." Then he closed the door and went back to the couch in the living room.

As Streets predicted, the Spartans lost their next game on Friday night, to Cape Nez. Citrus City played well, Powell ran well, Callahan's pass completion percentage was excellent. Up against a strong, veteran-filled team that had lost only two games, the score rocked back and forth. In the last few minutes of the fourth quarter, the Spartans went up by three points on a spectacular run by Franklin Powell.

Citrus City knew Cape Nez had been successful several times on sideline kickoff returns, and this had been emphasized by their scouts, so on the ensuing kickoff, they were ready for it. Cape Nez could be seen sending their blockers over to the sideline and the Citrus City defenders rushed to that side to foil the play. The trouble was, the Cape Nez runner, also one of the state's best sprinters, took the ball on his fifteen, started right, then cut back straight up the middle. He went eighty-five yards for a touchdown, then kicked the extra point. The Spartans and their supporters were stunned. There wasn't time for Citrus City to score again and the game ended, Cape Nez 35, Citrus City 31.

Streets didn't go to the game. He hadn't missed a Friday night game for years but he couldn't face the crowds or the team, so he stayed home. When he saw the scores on television, he was elated. He jumped and shouted, "I knew they couldn't do it without me!" He jumped up again and repeated what he had said.

The next day, Saturday morning, Streets went to see his mother, then hung around home waiting for the coaches to come beg him to come back to the team. He figured what he'd say to them. To Coach Warren, he would say, "Yeah, Whitey, you can't do it without me, can you?" Then he'd laugh in the sniveling coach's face. He might not act as smart-alecky to Coach Johnson, that was some evermore man, but he'd let him know who was the big wheel on the football team. They'd have to crawl to Streets.

When the morning wore on, first nine o'clock, then ten and eleven, Streets grew restless. Maybe the coaches had some other problems like injuries or something. By one o'clock when they hadn't come, Streets knew they weren't coming that day to beg him. They were probably too ashamed and embarrassed. His teammates didn't come either. Of course, he never was buddy-buddy with anybody but he was used to that. He felt it was because they didn't understand him either. When you were superior in every way, other people had to kowtow to you and that's just the way it was.

Sunday was a big problem to Streets. The coaches still didn't come begging him, and his teammates avoided him. He walked downtown again but there weren't many people hanging around and he could see a few who walked inside their houses or the stores when he approached and he couldn't understand that. He didn't go to church so it was easy to avoid those holier-than-thou people. He bought the Sunday paper and retreated to his house to read it and to watch football games, not caring who won nor whether they played at all. He went to see his mother, and when he was unusually quiet, she said to him, "Son, you're not sayin' much today. Is it because the football team lost that game?"

"Yes ma'am, I guess so."

Gertrude Jackson felt really good this morning, rested and full of good breakfast. She wasn't used to breakfast in bed nor to having white nurses' aides serve her, and she took a quiet mirthful pleasure in it. She had sure served a lot of white people, and it did her good to have it the other way around. Still, her strapping son's unusually withdrawn silence disturbed her. "Are you worried because the team might not git to be in the state championship playoffs?"

"Yeah, Momma, that's part of it, but you know the team can't win it without me, and the coaches haven't even been around to see me, to tell me how much they need me. I don't think they've got any sense about the only way they can win and they haven't even given me a call."

Streets was naive about other people's pride, but then he was naive about a lot of things. His constant introspection, his sense of his own importance insulated him from any empathy he might have otherwise had. He simply couldn't see things from any point of view other than his own.

"Son," Gertrude said, "Don't you know they're not goin' to come around and beg you to come back to the team? They can't do that because of their own pride and the pride of the team. Everybody knows you're good, but you're not the only one who's good and no matter how much talent you've got, there'll always be someone who comes along who's about as good as you, maybe even better. That's jus' the way it is. You know when you broke the hundred record, someone else held it and they had to be good too, so someone'll come along who'll break your record. It ain't that you're not a fine athalete, son, it's jus' that there's other boys who have a lot of ability too, so don't hang around waitin' for them coaches to beg you to play. They're not goin' to do it." It was a long speech for Gertrude, but it showed she'd put a lot of thought into her son's situation.

On the other side of town, I'd been doing a lot of thinking, too. I wasn't aware of the conversation Streets and his mother were having, but my mind was in turmoil. Losing the game to Cape Nez was a real blow to the team's efforts to get into the state playoffs. Now we were tied with Cape Nez for the district lead. We had to win the last regular season game, and they had to lose for us to get into the playoffs. I desperately wished I had Streets playing and that he hadn't had that temper tantrum. I didn't know if we could take him back on the team or not. Regardless of my feelings, I did owe that boy and his family the chance for a college scholarship, but his actions made it so hard to take him back on the team that we were in a quandary. I knew some of the players wanted him back because they'd worked so hard to get into the playoffs and they didn't care about whether we caved in to him, they still wanted his talent so we could have shot at the championship. He would sure have to do some apologizing to the team to get my vote. Powell had stepped in and done a great job, but we still needed Streets. Maybe we could win the state title without Streets but we'd be so much more potent with him.

The team was pretty confused. Some wanted Streets back at any cost, others didn't know if they wanted him back at all. I was glad the kids weren't split along racial lines on the question of Streets getting back on the team. Some of the black kids wanted him back, some didn't, and the same was true of the white kids. I sure wished I knew more of what was going on in Streets' mind.

When Streets returned from seeing his mother, he considered all she had said to him. He had never given much thought to whether or not his mother was wise but their conversation sure showed she could think some pretty complicated thoughts.

On Monday, he picked fruit instead of going to school so he wouldn't have to face the team or the coaches, and he didn't want to hear any remarks from the kids. Anyway, he could think while he picked fruit and still pick more than anyone else on the crew. He was agitated enough so he didn't mind rising up before dawn to meet the dented orange picking bus.

As they rode to the grove, he usually took pleasure from looking at the brilliant green of the trees, so green that they seemed almost artificial, and the contrasting orange and yellow fruit looked like it was daubed on the trees by an artist. On this forty degree November morning, his mind was not on the beauty of the trees. He took off his denim jacket when he left the bus because he knew he'd be warm as soon as he had picked the big canvas sack full of oranges.

They were working on an old grove with tall trees, a grove the burrowing nematode had not attacked, and they had to use twenty foot ladders. Streets saw some of the older, weaker men struggle with the ladders, but for him it was just a workout. There was an older man in his crew who weighed one hundred thirty pounds, who always picked fruit, and had a house full of children. It was all the man could do to move the big ladders; sometimes the younger, stronger men would help him. Streets knew the man drank a six pack of beer every night to get enough courage to show up at the grove the next day.

When Streets moved into the rhythm of picking, he could use both hands and still think about his football situation. He knew there were other good football players like his mother had said, but he began to think, if they were as good as he was, how come he could outrun all of them, and why had he scored more points than anyone else in the state before he left the team?

While Streets was moving his ladder, he saw the puny older man trying to jockey his huge ladder into position on the next tree. Streets said, "Here, Pop, let me handle that thing for you." The young athlete deftly swung the ladder around and levered it into position against the tree.

"Thanks, son, sometimes these things are mighty hard to handle. I used to do it pretty quick, but it ain't as easy as it used to be."

When he had climbed his ladder again, his thoughts turned back to the football team. Maybe Momma was wrong after all. He had always been better at everything in athletics than anyone he played against, so how could anyone be as good as him?

He thought to himself, the coaches are really wrong, but maybe they don't realize it, and my mother doesn't understand it either. I really am better and I was right to tell Coach Warren off. He was the one who was wrong. When you're the best, the team has to build itself around you and the coaches have to be careful how they treat you.

He thought about apologizing, but decided it was dumb. He thought they would eventually have to see how wrong they were and then they would come to try to get him back.

On Wednesday, Streets returned to school. He knew he'd have to face the other students and the team members sooner or later, and he had to stay eligible to play, just in case. He had walked the ten blocks in a light rain, dressed in a good-looking London Fog raincoat he had bought at the Goodwill store for five dollars. He carried no books because he rarely took them home since he could do enough work at school to pass, and he could see absolutely no reason for someone who was going to play in the National Football League to excel in school work.

He was oblivious to the splendid architecture of his high school, the spread out buildings and covered walkways, the well-planned landscaping, the greens and reds and yellows of the plants. What he thought about was Streets Jackson.

When Streets walked down the hallway, a space opened up for him as if he were in a bubble. Everyone knew of his expulsion from the team and the standoff between him and the coaches. His team members spoke to him but remained aloof. Wednesday and Thursday passed without any overture from the coaches and he couldn't understand it. Didn't they see how dumb they were not to come on their knees to him?

On Friday night, the Spartans played the last regular game of the season against Riverport. Streets was determined not to apologize to the team or the coaches. It wasn't his part to apologize for something that wasn't his fault. They were wrong and he was right, so why should he apologize? They had lost the previous game without him so they knew how valuable he was and that they couldn't win without him. Boy, were they stupid. If they'd just had sense enough to apologize to him and beg him to come back, maybe he would have given them the privilege of having him back. It hurt not to be playing but he did have his pride.

It was mid-November, a cold forty-five degrees at the Memorial Stadium. The Spartans took the field without Streets, against a Riverport team that had won five and lost four. Riverport was a young team, brilliant at times and mediocre at others. Citrus City was solid at every position, good on both defense and offense. Not having Streets affected their ability to run the score up quickly, but did not take away from their fine balance and expertise at nearly every position. With the veteran quarterback Callahan passing, fast ends and pass catching backs, and the bruising play of Horst Michler and Hunky King, they could not be denied another victory. They spanked Riverport and sent them home on the short end of a 30 to 7 score, while Cape Nez lost to Sharpton. The good news was that they were in the state playoffs. The bad news was that they had to face an unbeaten team, Ridgecrest from Orlando which had a 10-0 record.

Gertrude Jackson went home from the hospital on Saturday morning after the Riverport game, making the family excited and very happy. Although they would have a hard time expressing it, they had their rock back in their lives, and the brothers and sisters had another authority. Taking orders from Streets was a tough proposition. Saturday went smoothly, the children cleaned up the house to please their mother, even did their lessons without being told. Streets picked fruit again which made his mother happy, but when Jonathan told her that Streets was still at odds with the coaches and the team, she was terribly upset.

When Streets came through the door at 5:30 that afternoon, Gertrude was ready for him. "Son, you' not back on that football team yet?"

"No, ma'am."

"How come?"

"Mama, they still don't understand. Coach Warren was wrong to kick me off and I don't feel like it's my place to 'pologize to him or the team. They' got a bad attitude."

Gertrude was furious. "Now you listen to me, boy. I thought we had this thing all thrashed out the other day up in the hospital. The coich is not the one who is wrong, you are. You think you so almighty wonderful and you ain't. God blessed you with a fantastic body and because you're body's made you into a good athalete, you think you' God's gift to the worl." Her eyes spit fire as she stood over the sulking Streets. "God shoulda give it to some boy who would appreciate it instead of a conceited stuck-up person like you. You had a chance to git a collidge scholarship and maybe help the family some, and you throwin' it down the drain outta pride." With this emotional outburst, Gertrude collapsed to the floor, hitting her head on the arm of the couch as she fell.

Streets was scared beyond reason. He ran next door to the Wiggins' house and called 911. The ambulance was at the front door in ten minutes, and though Streets shook his mother gently and tried to bring her back to consciousness, she never moved a muscle.

Gertrude, back in intensive care, refused to come out of her coma. The doctors, sure it must be a stroke, put her through the necessary test, but would not give a diagnosis until they knew more. A contrite Streets, sitting in the sterile waiting room, prayed like a soldier at the front. He told God, "Lord, if you'll just bring my Momma back to us, I'll do anything. I'll go to church, I'll study hard, I'll apologize to the coach and the team, I'll do anything. Jus' please, let us have our Momma."

Streets stayed at the hospital all Saturday night, all Sunday and Sunday night while his brothers and sisters took turns being with him and sleeping at home. He gave them no orders but let them make up their minds what they wanted to do.

When there had been no change by Monday morning, Streets decided he'd make his mother happier by going to school than by staying home or being near her at the hospital. It was to be a very emotional day for Streets. There was so much he had to do to try to get back in his mother's and God's good graces.

Streets showed up at my office when I put my key in the door. Without any pretense at formality, he said, "Coach, I got to talk to you. How bout if I come back third period?"

Not knowing what to expect, I told the athlete, "Sure, Streets. Is it something you can't tell me right now?"

"No sir. I need more than a few minutes to say what's on my mind, so if you don't care, I'll come back third period."

Streets knew he had some work to make up, and as soon as his first period class door was open, he was in his seat, bent over his textbook, studying intently. He was polite to the students around him but not effusive. A tiger can't change his stripes. He paid careful attention to the teachers, writing down assignments, thinking what he must do to get better grades.

When third period rolled around, Streets asked Coach Tucker if he could be excused from math class so he could talk to me. Bearing a hall pass, Streets walked swiftly to my office.

As soon as he was seated, Streets blurted out, "Coach, I've made some terrible mistakes and I want to try to correct 'em."

"You're right about that, son. Suppose you tell me what you're thinking."

"Well, first of all, it's my momma, Coach. You know she got hurt in that car wreck. Well, she got out of the hospital and came home, but I made her so mad, she fainted and hit her head. Now she's back in the hospital and it's my fault. She tried to tell me I was wrong about you and the team and first I thought maybe she was right but then I got to thinkin' that I was more valuable than she knew. I know I've got a mean streak in me and I know I'm a good athlete so maybe I think too much of myself. I sure do need my momma to get well and my whole family does, so I guess I've got God mad at me too. Maybe I can straighten things out if I only know where to start."

I was glad to hear such a confession from this troubled kid. He had it all pegged about right. His mother's original injury was not his fault, but surely it was his fault that she fainted when she was so mad at him. We all hoped it wasn't a stroke because there were so many who depended on her.

"Coach, I know I shouldn't cuss," the repentant Streets said. "I was wrong to talk back to you that day at practice, and you know sometimes I'm a conceited jerk. I do apologize to you and I'm really sorry; it's not just somethin' I think I should say to be back in with you. You were right to put me off the team and I'da done the same as you if I was in your place. I've let the team down big time, maybe even caused 'em to lose, and I'm so sorry for that, you can't know how bad I feel. If you'll even consider letting me talk to the team, I'm beggin' you. I don't know if they want me back or not, and I wouldn't blame 'em if they didn't. I sure have thought all about me and not at all about them."

Taking Streets back on the team was a big decision, too big for me. The team had to be a part of the decision and the other coaches had to be involved. It wasn't just a matter of saying to Streets that he was back on the team and all was forgiven. To forgive was one thing, to forget another, because he had stretched us to the limit. I told him, "Come down to the field at 5:30 this afternoon and I'll call the team together so you can talk to them. Then, after practice is over, I'd like for you to talk to the coaching staff. I'm not promising a thing except that we'll listen to what you have to say."

I could tell it sounded pretty tough to Streets but I didn't really care, I had to put the feelings of the team and the coaches first. The team had hung together with great character whether or not they ever became state champions. I guess to someone for whom high school athletics was not important, our situation might seem childish, but for us coaches and the team members who had put in hundreds, sometimes thousands of hours, the drive toward the state championship was an all-absorbing ambition. Sure, ten years from now this might not seem so important, but for now, it occupied every minute of our thoughts.

I'd like to have been with Streets, to know what was going on inside his fertile brain. As he went through his day's schedule, Streets floated as if in a daze. He paid almost no attention to the other students, speaking when spoken to, not seeking out any companionship. He was unusually attentive in class, working his math problems, reading his assignments, and listening with concentration to his teachers.

Practice went smoothly that afternoon and 5:30 came quickly. I called the team together and got them down on one knee with Streets standing near me. They all knew what the meeting was about. I looked around at the talent that surrounded me knowing that many scholarships would be offered to the athletes on this team. I was carried back to the first day of practice when the coaches looked over the team and decided they looked more like a small college team than a high school team. They really were mature with the line averaging well over two hundred pounds on both offense and defense. The explosiveness of Hunky King and the huge rangy savageness of Horst Michler were so apparent that the most unobserving person could see it.

Without any preliminaries, I told the team that Streets had asked to talk to them.

He was more hesitant than I had ever seen him. He said, "You' been my team members for all my life, and even if I've not been a very good friend to most of you, I'd like to call you my friends. I' been very selfish, seein' football and the other sports from only my own point of view. I guess I see everything from only the way it affects me. I've been so rude to the coaches, I don't see how they could put up with me for five minutes." With this, he ducked his head and no eloquent speaker ever had the attention of his audience more than Streets did on this chilly afternoon.

"First of all, I want to 'pologize to Alfonius 'cause I hit him for no reason at all and he's been my buddy all my life. I want to 'pologize to the whole team for letting you all down when maybe I could have helped you, although with my attitude, I don't know if I could have helped anybody. My attitude stinks and I guess it always has. I hope I can change that, at least it's somethin' I intend to do."

"I've got to tell you, I resented Franklin Powell for bein' able to step in and take my place when I should have been glad for the team and for Franklin. I'm glad I don't have to be the linebacker on the other side when he comes through a hole. What I'm sayin' to you is this. I'd like to play with you again even though I know I don't deserve it but I leave it up to you. If you don't want me back, I can understand because if I were you, I wouldn't want me back either."

At the end of his speech, Streets stepped back behind Coach Caleb Johnson. The team ran wind sprints and went in.

The palm trees blew in the November wind, and the practice field grass, worn from thousands of grinding cleats, turned its sparse face toward the graying sky as we drifted back toward the locker rooms.

Streets followed us as we filed into my crowded office, into a tension-filled atmosphere. Everyone but Streets and I settled into one of the scarred brown metal chairs and I gave him the floor. I had been impressed by what he had said to the assembled team but that wasn't enough.

He started out, "To you men who are my coaches, I can't tell you how grateful I am to have landed at a high school which has so many good coaches who are also good men. I know a lot of schools end up with either good coaches or bad coaches and good or bad men. Us boys haven't known how lucky we are. For me to talk back to Coach Warren is ridiculous and now I know it. I guess I didn't really know it before. You all know my mother got hurt in that wreck and was unconscious for days, and she finally came out of it and was able to come home. She told me I was wrong about thinkin' Coach Warren shouldn't have kicked me off the team and that I thought too much of my own self."

"Still, in my own mind, I was the one who was right because I thought I was so good you coaches should do it my way. After my mother was home and found out I hadn't apologized to you and to the team, she was so mad she screamed at me and she fainted and hit her head again. Now she's back in the hospital and I don't know if she'll come out of it or not. I guess I even take her for granted, too. Nobody ever had a better mother, and my brothers and sisters and me, we're all realizin' it now. Her gettin' better is more important to me than the football team or anythin' else in my life. I wanted to tell you coaches this so you'd know what changed my thinkin'.

"I've only given you a hundred percent when it's to my advantage, I been a poor student, and even though God gave me a good body, I haven't appreciated it except that it's made other people think I was a good athlete. I love for the newspapers to write my name in the headlines, and I like for people to point at me on the street and tell each other how good I am. What I'm sayin' is this. I don't deserve to be back on the team. Anyhow, I'd like to get another chance and I promise if I do, I'll make you proud of me in a different way than you were before. I think God's tryin' to punish me and I don't blame Him either. I guess that's about all I have to say."

I told Streets I'd talk to the team again the next day and get back to him. We coaches talked at some length about Streets. We all felt terrible about Gertrude Jackson and I knew Caleb had his church people praying fervently for her.

Speedy let us know what he was thinking when he said, "You guys know how great it is to have a sprinter like Streets who is the fastest dash man in the state, and how much he means to my track program as well as to our football team. Still, I think we owe it to the team to let them decide if they want him back or not. He really has let them down and they all know it."

I called a team meeting the next day in the middle school auditorium across the street. Our school was nice and new but the school board didn't have the money for a regular auditorium so we had to use the one which was in the middle school building.

I told the team, "What we say here must not go any farther than this room, no matter how much people ask you about it. If your friends ask you, just tell them it was a private meeting and let it go at that, and if you're as mature as I think you are, you can keep it to yourself. Also, Streets must never know what we say here."

They had talked it over thoroughly. They were amazed as all of us were at what Streets had said and they wondered if it could last. Alfonius Jefferson had accepted Streets' apology but I knew he still bore some resentment. Hunky King probably put it best when he stated, "I've grown up with Streets and I've seen his temper a thousand times. He hurts people and doesn't seem to care and that bothers me a lot, but I've never seen him act like this before. I think his apology to us is real, totally sincere, and I tell you, I don't understand it. He's never been like this before. Maybe it's because of his mother, and if it is, it might wake him up. I'm in favor of taking him back on the team, but if we do, I sure want to see a different attitude from him."

The upshot of it was that we took Streets back on the team. When he reported for practice that day, I left Franklin Powell running with the first team and Streets running with the second team, but he didn't say a word. I knew what I was doing was strange, putting him on the second team. I doubted if he had ever been on the second team in anything his whole life. If he resented it, we were never to know. He didn't say much but he sure didn't tell anybody what to do either.

The team looked good. Those same physiques we had observed on the first day of practice still stood out all across the team. They were surely finer tuned. Only a very few had gained any weight since August although we were still lifting three days a week. Weightlifting is a wonderful thing in a way because it's usually a weight reducer to the fatter kids and a weight gainer to the ones who need muscle. Franklin surely looked good running with the first team. His six foot four and two forty put him a half head taller and bigger than most of the boys and he really filled out that uniform. He hadn't been a runner on the track team, so we really didn't know exactly how fast he might be. What was liable to happen was that some colleges would want to recruit him and then convert him to the line which is where he was so unsuccessful.

The air was cold and it started to rain, one of those fast moving rains that would be over in a few minutes. I didn't want the boys to get soaked so I sent them in. The flu season had hit and if several of our key player were out with the flu, we might lose the first playoff game to Ridgecrest. I'd seen coaches play their athletes even though they had the flu, and somehow the boys would usually play well, but

I didn't see how they could do it and I sure didn't want to be in that position.

I told them, "Take a good hot shower, be sure your hair is dry before you start home, don't stay around anyone who is sick, and don't kiss your girlfriend if she has a cold. If fact, lay off of that kissing stuff, it messes up your mind." They laughed at this but I was dead serious.

# 22

# The Change

GERTRUDE JACKSON CAME OUT OF HER COMA on Wednesday. A nurse called me at home to tell me about overhearing the meeting between Gertrude and Streets. She said when he went into the intensive care unit and saw that her eyes were open, he took her hand and knelt down beside the bed and wept.

He said, "Momma, I'm so glad you're awake again, and I want you to know I've sorta got things straightened out. We need you, Momma, me and the other kids. Whatever it takes to be sure you get better, that's what we'll do."

Gertrude's tired eyes looked at her strapping son as her face drifted into a tiny smile and she said, "Son, I need you too, but I need you to do what's right so's we can have things go along smooth. Are you straightened out down at the school house?"

"Yes ma'am, I think so. I told the coaches and the team how sorry I was that I was such a jerk. Momma, I didn't know really how bad I was 'til you made me see it, and I feel like I've changed. I sure hope so. I 'pologized to the team and to the coaches and they let me back on the football team. They got me playin' second string and you know I ain't used to that, but I don't care, if they'll just let me play, maybe I can show 'em that I can be valuable to the team."

"How you really feelin' Momma?"

"I don' know, Son. I jus' feel so tired, that's all. I still got me a headache but it seems a little bit better, and they takin' good care of me. I sure thank God for the company insurance."

The sterile room, the humming of the monitors, the nurses busy checking the seriously ill in the big room, all were shut out from Streets and his mother as they talked quietly. He smiled at his mother. "Momma, I'm goin' home and fix supper for the kids. They bein' real good and they gonna be so glad you' conscious again. I'll get 'em to do their homework and then I'll let some of 'em come see you for a few minutes. Things are gonna be better, Momma, you wait and see."

# 23

# First Playoff Game Ridgecrest

Just to get our attention, Orlando Ridgecrest threw a pass on the first play from scrimmage, and their split end scored without ever being touched. They kicked the point and the score read, Ridgecrest 7, Citrus City 0. I didn't think I had any heart trouble but I sure had a funny feeling in my chest.

This team was everything their record indicated. They had scored more points than any other team, and they showed no sign of overconfidence. They had been second to us in the state track meet last year and had plenty of speed left from that team. Their linebackers were about two hundred fifteen pounds apiece, they had a marvelous coaching staff, and they were veterans in the state playoffs. They had been here before.

I started Powell instead of Streets, though I knew the grandstand quarterbacks were raking me over the coals pretty good for that one. How do you sit the fastest player in the state on the bench in favor of someone who has only played in the backfield for a few weeks? Still, I felt I had to do it. Streets had put us through some hard times, and Franklin had surely come through for us. I regretted not having seen a year or so earlier that Franklin would be a good back.

Our scouting reports and the films we had seen on them showed that Ridgecrest's weakest spot seemed to be a fairly young defensive secondary, so we came out throwing. Callahan was good and I meant to take every advantage of his arm. We started with short passes, first to the sideline because they're so hard to defend against, then as soon as we had made the defenders sideline conscious, we popped a couple of short passes over the center. When we called on Powell to drive the ball through the line, he banged up in there really good, but those big linebackers would only give him three or four yards at a time, and that was on the good plays.

We moved the ball to the fifty, then Powell fumbled and Ridgecrest recovered. They got as far as our thirty when Streets intercepted one of their passes and ran it back up to the fifty again before someone lowered the boom on him. At least he didn't throw his helmet or blame someone for not blocking him. The score still read seven to nothing in their favor and all of Citrus City was terribly worried. Our offense ran onto the field and Streets came off with the defense. From the grandstand there were cries of "Put Streets in there, meathead," and other such complimentary yells.

Franklin banged up to the forty-eight for a gain of two. Buck passed to our tight end over the center for a gain of five, down to the forty-three. I sent in instructions for Buck to call for the screen pass and it worked for ten yards, down to the thirty-three. Things were looking up and the fans screamed their approval. We drove the ball to the seven, and using Franklin straight into the line as a decoy, Buck handed the ball to Johnny Blocker who slanted off right tackle to score. We all breathed a sigh of relief, then Matt Priest missed the extra point. Seven to six in favor of Ridgecrest.

It rocked on like that right up to the middle of the third quarter. I put Streets in the ball game for Franklin, thinking he might break loose with his dynamic running but nothing special happened. He was tentative, acting like he was not sure of himself. I really couldn't understand it, seeing Streets Jackson unsure of himself as he had never been in his life. On offense he played like a sophomore who had seldom been in a ball game and not like the state hundred meter champion. He was adequate, but just barely.

We traded scores with Ridgecrest twice more until, in the middle of the fourth quarter, the score read Ridgecrest 21, Citrus City 20. It began to look like the oft-repeated line, "Maybe next year, Coach."

We came to the time when there were only three minutes left and Ridgecrest was driving into our territory. They did one of those things that cause coaches to turn gray and lose their jobs. They were ahead, and with the clock running down, their quarterback threw a pass right into the arms of Matt Priest and he made up for the missed extra point by running the ball sixty-five yards for a touchdown. He made this extra point and we won 27 to 21.

In the bedlam that followed, we were all elated. It wasn't perfect and it left us all a little shaken. The band played like John Philip Sousa was leading them, and the fans were hysterical. The rest of the team screamed and laughed but I noticed Streets was not taking part in the celebration. I thought maybe he was going to blow up on us again.

When I talked to his math teacher Bruce Tucker on Tuesday, I asked him about Streets and received a disturbing answer. "He seems to be okay, Coach, but he's mighty quiet. There's something going on in that boy's head that's different than anything I've seen from him before. He's more interested in his schoolwork, if that's any comfort to you, but again I say, he's mighty quiet. Too quiet."

I asked Bruce about his love life and he laughed. "You mean about my dates with Natalie Shires?"

"Yeah, I mean about your dates with Natalie Shires, unless you've suddenly started dating three or four women and not told us about them."

Bruce pushed his glasses up on his nose and laughed again. "We've been out several times, Angus, and I really like her. She's surely not been around much and I like that too. I even had her over to my house for dinner and let the kids fix it. They were a little uncertain seeing me have an interest in someone other than their mother, but they liked Natalie. She was pleasant to them but she didn't come on too strong and I guess that's easier to take than if she had gushed at them. She has a mother who is a pistol and really doesn't want me near her darling daughter. She must think I have leprosy or something."

"Bruce, I'm confident you and Natalie can work it out. I hope so, because I like that girl."

I told Bruce I'd see him later and retreated to my hole in the gym. When they made my schedule, they gave me two planning periods rather than one, since I was the athletic director as well as the head football coach. I needed the extra time to take phone calls and order equipment and handle the thousand little details that come up. My four

English classes kept me busy enough even without the football and my mind was easily distracted during football season. It's always easy for a coach to get so interested in coaching and winning that he neglects his academic classes, and I tried to guard against that.

I still wished I knew what was going on in Street's mind, not that I'd know what to do if he caused another problem. I knew if he tried to tell us coaches what to do again, I'd have to kick him off the team permanently and that would be the end of it.

I might have felt better if I'd known what had gone on at Streets' house after his mother went home from the hospital.

# CALEB AND THE JACKSONS

"GO TO CHURCH? MOMMA, WHATTA' YOU talkin' about? I don't want to go to no church!" Jonathan was adamant. They had never been to church and he obviously couldn't see any sense in it.

Gertrude looked tired and more frail than her children had seen her. "Well maybe it's about time we did go, Jonathan, we sho' need to change somethin' about the way we're livin'."

It was a Saturday evening and they had just finished a big meal of spaghetti and fresh baked bread. The children felt happy and contented with having their mother home, and they were all silently glad that Streets wasn't telling them what to do all the time. He sat at the other end of the table from his mother, a throne from which he often reigned, but tonight he hadn't hassled them at all.

After listening to the bickering between Jonathan and Gertrude, Streets quietly said, "I guess we better go, Jonathan; it sure can't hurt none and it might help us somehow. You remember we told God we'd do anything if Momma got better and now I guess we better keep our promise. He sure must like for people to go to church."

When the Jackson family showed up at Coach Johnson's church, one could almost see the big preacher-coach's heart swell. The Jackson's filled up an entire row of seats and the deacons fell all over themselves pumping Gertrude and Streets' hands and right down to the littlest hand. Caleb tried not to make too much of their presence as he didn't want to drive them away with the enthusiasm of the welcome.

As he shook hands with them at the door, looking like one of the prophets of old, Caleb couldn't help but impress the Jackson family.

When he released Caleb's hand, Streets asked him, "Coach, is it okay if I come back and talk to you some?"

"Why sure Streets, I told you that before; you can always come and talk to me anytime about anything. There's a whole lot I don't know, but I've had a lot of experience talkin' to people." He laughed as he said it, his voice echoing in the vestibule of the church. "Could you come to my house this afternoon about two o'clock, after I've had time for my dinner?"

"Sure, Coach, that'd be fine."

They were a small army, the Jackson family, as they made their way back to the house by the railroad tracks. The other children went ahead of Streets and his mother, the younger ones running, showing promise of the coordination with which their older brother ran.

"What do you want to talk to Coach Johnson about, son?" With his apparent mellowing, Gertrude felt confident he wouldn't get mad at her for asking, something she would not have done some weeks before.

"Momma, there's a whole lot of things I need to talk to him about. I think he's the right one. I ain't never had no interest in goin' to church before, but I think God's mad at me and I want to know what to do to make Him feel better toward me."

"Also, about college. I guess I've made the universities take another look at me and they may not like what they see."

When he showed up at Coach Johnson's house at two o'clock, Streets quickly opened the conversation. "How come God's so mad at me coach?"

"What d'you mean, Streets?"

"Everything bad's happenin' to me at once, Coach. I mean, my Momma got hurt and I got kicked off the football team. It just seems like bad things are pilin' up on me. I know I never paid any attention to the church or to God, and I guess He's just showin' me who's boss."

"I don't think God works that way, son. He knows everything we do, and He must be very unhappy with us when we do things that are wrong, but I don't think He pays us back for not doin' things His way. He makes the rain fall on the just and the unjust."

"What does that mean?"

"It means that good things happen to bad people and bad things happen to good people, too."

"Well how come these things are happenin' to me?"

The big coach rubbed his short chin whiskers, leaned back in his chair, and said, "I'm sure glad you're takin' a look at yourself, Streets, 'cause you've made most of your own troubles. You already said it yourself when you talked to the football team. You mostly just think of yourself and you're very mean to other people. God blessed you with a wonderful body and you've thought it was just you who was so wonderful. If you'll look around you and see the boys who have to struggle so hard to try to be on the football team or any other team, you'll see that there's some of them who'd give anything to be a star or even just to be good at somethin'. It all comes so easy to you it's made you think too much of yourself."

Streets squirmed in his chair. "Well, what about my momma. I didn't make her have that wreck."

The big coach stood up and paced. "You sure didn't, son, and don't you take the blame for that." He paused and then continued, "But you sure hurt her when you didn't do what she asked you to." He stood still in the center of the room for a moment. "You're bigger and older than your brothers and sisters, but you must be more mature. You've got some growin' up to do, and I don't mean physically. Like you said, God can't be very pleased with someone who takes his body for granted like he invented it, by someone who goes around poppin' people on the chin when he doesn't like the way they do things, by someone who struts around the town like a proud rooster, by someone who puts himself above all others."

The lithe athlete hesitated a moment before he spoke. "What about this college thing, Coach. D'you think I've ruined my chance at a scholarship?"

Coach Johnson smiled. "Like we've been sayin', son, God blessed you with a wonderful body and lots of ability. I'm sure you'll have your chance to go to college on an athletic scholarship, but you haven't helped it any by bein' thrown off the team for a while. All the recruiters know about it and if there's anything they don't need at these colleges, it's temperamental players who think they have to have their own way. When you start receivin' those scholarship offers, I want you to come back and talk to me about them. You have to choose the school that's best for your future, even though it might not look that way at first."

Streets sat for a moment with his head down. "Coach, I'm gonna come to church and listen to you some, 'cause I don't think God's through with me. I don't think I ever listened to a sermon before, but maybe I ought to. There's sure a whole lot I've got to think about."

When Coach Johnson opened the door to let Streets out, he surely felt a great satisfaction, knowing that whether his sermon this morning hadn't reached anyone, and even if much of the good he tried to do went without any apparent result, today he had watched someone take a step forward.

# 25

# NATALIE AND BRUCE

THE CLOSING BELL HAD RUNG, THE LAST CLASS had departed, and Natalie Shires was straightening her room. She always picked up any paper on the floor as she didn't want the custodians to tell principal Seidthorn she was messy. She found that the floor could be perfectly clean, but that the minute a teacher turned her back to write something on the board, many pieces of paper could suddenly appear on the floor as if by magic. From spotless clean to a ticker tape parade in a moment of time.

Like most school rooms, hers was adequate. The school board kept it painted and air-conditioned against the muggy months and there was room for thirty-five chairs, but you couldn't play tennis in the extra space.

She had history papers to grade, and as she put a rubber band around them, the ever more welcome face of Bruce Tucker appeared in the doorway. At first, Natalie had been very happy to have Bruce ask her for date, but she was realistic enough not to expect too much from him. They had been out several times and what was at first fun and companionship had changed to contented togetherness, from holding hands of which she had done very little, to escalating kisses of which she had done even less. Now, the sight of the tall easygoing math teacher made her a little weak. She had stopped thinking of their relationship as just companionable and hoped fervently that he could love her as she now loved him. She realized that Bruce knew more about kisses and sex than she did, surely a lot more about sex, and this made her weaker.

She saw Bruce as kind, noble, and brilliant; truly a knight come to rescue her from the wicked witch in the castle. Bruce wasn't quite the superman wonder she made him, and her mother wasn't the wicked witch although she had done everything in her power to break up the budding romance.

Natalie's mother had consented to meet Bruce when he came to pick up Natalie for her third date. "You're just infatuated because some man's finally paid you some attention," her mother said. "I guess I'd better inspect him, Natalie, so I can tell you what's wrong with him, because with your head in the clouds, you couldn't possibly be any judge of him."

Amanda was having a bad hair day when they had this conversation. Looking at her mother, Natalie saw her hair a little wild, watched her spitting out the words with eyes emitting sparks, and thought the word witch. Witch! Immediately, Natalie was ashamed because usually her mother was nice, but the older lady surely didn't want her meal ticket, her support for the present soft life, to be stolen from her.

Amanda could find no redeeming quality in Bruce. He was older than Natalie, he was too thin, he had children who would always be a burden; the list of his faults was endless. Recounting these did nothing to stem Natalie's ardor, only elevating him another notch or two.

When Bruce walked into the room, she greeted him and was surprised when he walked into the darkest corner of the room. "Come over here a minute, Natalie, I've something I want to tell you."

When she walked to where he was, Bruce pulled her to him and kissed her thoroughly. Natalie was frightened, looking desperately at the windows and the doorway. "Oh, Bruce, don't do that here!" She put her hand on his arm, saying, "It's not that I don't want you to kiss me, but what if Mr. Seidthorn should walk in. I haven't had this job very long and I sure don't want to lose it."

Bruce laughed. "I never heard of a teacher getting the ax for kissing another teacher. If we were both married to someone else, old thorn in the side might have something to holler about, but I don't see any real harm in it." He smiled and added, "Besides, I've been thinking about doing that all day, and you taste good." He looked thoughtful. "Still, if it bothers you, I promise not to do it again. I mean here at school. Otherwise, I make no promises." Bruce walked her to her car and he made arrangements to pick her up for the ball game on Friday night.

When she told her mother of her Friday night date, a frantic look came on Amanda's face. "I've told you I don't want you going with that man, Natalie. Nothing good can come of it and you're just throwing yourself at him, and that's that."

On Friday, Amanda took to her bed with elevated blood pressure and an actors display of illness. Bruce went to the ball game without Natalie.

# 26

# State Playoff Semi-final Game Miami Saint Paul

A THOUSAND THOUGHTS SWIRLED THROUGH my head as I drove from my home toward the gym, thinking mostly about tonight's game with the Saints from Miami. They were talented, rugged, and quick and they had lost only one game in the tough Miami district. They were a polyglot of nationalities, made up of immigrants from Cuba, Nicaragua, Brazil, Mexico, you name it, plus the players from the big black population of Miami. There weren't more than a half dozen Anglos on the team, which is what we'd come to expect from the Miami which was no longer much of an Anglo town. Some considered the blacks to be the world's best athletes, and the immigrants wanted desperately to excel at something, so the combination was a real potent force.

I was still deeply concerned about Streets and how he might play. He seemed to me to be a smoldering volcano waiting to erupt and I couldn't trust him not to. He had given us absolutely no trouble at practice, still he wasn't the bruising running back he had been, though you couldn't put your finger on any action showing he was a slacker. The teachers reported that he was really studying more than he had ever done before, and that he was not a behavior problem, acting more like a quiet honor society member than an egocentric athlete. Maybe this taming down to be a student instead of an athlete was taking some of the fire he needed to be an explosive football player.

Driving along the palm-lined streets, I passed the massive pink concrete block hospital where Gertrude Jackson had gone through her two crises. I saw the band members in their uniforms, making their way toward the band room for their evening performance.

As I parked my Chevy, Speedy met me with some disturbing news. "We've got two kids out with the flu, Angus. It's Johnny Blocker and Hunky King."

I'd have been happier if he'd hit me over the head with a two-by-four and said that the players were all well. It was one of the problems a coach faces where he has no recourse; the ball game must go on whether the coach has all his horses or not. I could get along without Blocker by playing Powell for him, with Streets at the tailback slot. There was no way I could replace King.

I told Speedy, "Thanks for the bad apples," and walked into the dressing rooms to see how everyone else was doing. The taping was going on and it was a little quieter than usual. I saw Streets, half-dressed, waiting until everyone else was taped before he sat on one of the tables. The smell of the tape was always pungent and I believed that if you put me blindfolded into a dressing room anywhere, I'd know the smells of football uniforms.

I called Streets and Franklin over and explained the situation to them. "Tonight, Franklin, you're going to run fullback in place of Johnny Blocker, and Streets, you'll be in your regular halfback spot. Franklin, I know you haven't been running fullback lately, but you've run it enough in practice that it shouldn't be hard to get used to. I sure hate to make these switches in a playoff game but we don't have any choice." Streets didn't say a word but I assumed he was happy to be running first-string offense again.

When we lined up for the kickoff, I looked at the size of the Saint Paul players and felt my belly cramp because they must have outweighed us almost twenty pounds per man. I had never seen a high school team that big; it was no wonder they had lost only one game.

We kicked off to Saint Paul and they quickly showed us what their game plan was, which was to ram the ball down our throats, keeping it on the ground most of the time, using passes only to keep us honest. Coach Johnson changed his defenses as often as he saw a pattern develop, and they sure didn't push us around. You could tell Hunky King wasn't in there, because they could get a yard or two he'd never have allowed them. We held them on the first series of downs, then took over the ball and tried to move against them. Streets ran the ball a couple of times, still looking like he wasn't sure of himself, then Franklin ran it twice, fumbling the second time he ran it, not having the timing down from the fullback slot. They recovered the fumble on our forty-three, and having seen them run plays into our line, our linebackers socked it in there pretty tight, and they ran a post pattern that scored the first touchdown of the night. The point was good and they led us seven to zip. I hated to start another playoff game with the opponent scoring first.

We didn't get into the state playoffs by being a second class football team that was just lucky. Buck Callahan, as good as any quarterback in the state, sure of a scholarship from a big school, had led us for three years and now did for us what he was trained to do. He read the Saint Paul defenses, changed the play at the line of scrimmage if necessary, and gave us all a lesson in moving the football. He and I worked together. Our coach manning the headphones in the tower at the side of the field told me when he would see a weakness and I sent in plays to hit that weakness.

Buck started with short passes, easier to complete. He threw the sideline passes, throwing the ball away if it looked like it might be intercepted because we sure didn't need to see one of their fast defenders running down the sideline for a cheap touchdown. He completed enough of the short ones to move the ball relentlessly toward the Saints' goal line. We ran Franklin through the line often enough to keep them from keying on our receivers. Twice we ran the screen pass. Buck ran hooks with Marty Oliver when he would run past the defender, then come back quickly for two or three yards and get the perfectly timed pass from Callahan. As soon as he had the defender guarding Marty too closely, Buck sent him on the hook and go pattern and the athlete, one of our sprinters who could run the hundred in blue chip time, caught the ball and took it for a touchdown. Marty then kicked the extra point and we were tied at seven seven. The saints came back, taking advantage of Hunky King's absence. When they started pounding Hunky's linebacker spot, I moved Streets up from the deep defender's spot, cutting off their ability to pound that part of the line. Streets showed signs of his old brilliance, crunching their backs to the ground with the ferocity for which he was known. They tried running the ends with moderate success, Coach Johnson changing his defense when it looked like they might overpower us in one area. I feared they'd pick up Streets' move away from the deep defensive spot, and they eventually did. Their flanker ran toward the right sideline and Morton stayed just behind him. Instantly, I thought Morton was too close and the Saints flanker cut back very fast toward the goalposts, catching Morton flat-footed. The flanker caught the ball over his left shoulder and scored, sending the Saint Paul crowd into a frenzy. They kicked the extra point and led us 14 to 7.

I had just a minute with our offense before the kickoff, telling them to keep their heads up, not to get discouraged because there was a lot of ball game left. I saw Streets in the back of the other players with his head down and I wished I knew what he was thinking. I found out quickly as he took the kickoff back for a touchdown. I thanked God because it looked like Streets' old viciousness was back where it belonged, in the football game. On the extra point, Matt Priest booted the ball straight through the uprights to make it 14 to 14. I hated this kind of ball game, where the score rocked back and forth, with one of us in the lead and then the other, especially in a case like this where we had not yet been in the lead. We were hanging on by our fingernails.

On the next series, Callahan committed an error he almost never did. He backed away from the center before he had the ball well in his hands, dropping it to the turf where an alert Saint Paul nose guard covered it in an instant. Our defense held them like the champions we wanted to be, but Larsen was too keyed up, twice jumping offside, costing us ten yards in penalties, keeping alive their drives which would have died. They threw a deep pass and Benny Wells knocked the potential receiver down, costing us another penalty. We had shot ourselves four times on one drive, and it resulted in another Saints touchdown. When they kicked the extra point, I felt myself break into a cold sweat. Hello Saints twenty-one, Spartans fourteen, goodbye state title.

After the half, they kicked off to us and we drove the ball back to our own forty-five before we had to punt. I had preached to the team all year that if we were behind in a ball game, not to be discouraged because much of the time, if the other team has the ball, they will lose it with their own mistakes, just as we had done in the last series. We hung in there. We had to because they drove it down and kicked a forty-five-yard field goal. I hadn't seen many from that distance in high school and it was discouraging.

Buck Callahan's class showed through the whole game. He passed us down to their thirty-four despite their pounding him on almost every play. In the middle of the fourth quarter, Buck didn't get up after one of their rushes. Our team doctor and I ran out to him and found him holding his ankle. As we helped him to the sidelines, you could hear our fans groan for half a mile. I had to replace Buck with a junior quarterback, Charles Turkley, that the kids had quickly nicknamed Turkey. He was Turkey in the first grade and from then on, and he was so used to it that it never bothered him. It was not a complimentary name, but we learned he was no turkey because he had led the jayvees to two unbeaten seasons, looking like the next fine varsity quarterback. Turkey took over like Dan Marino, passing us to a touchdown with seven minutes left. True to our luck for the game, Priest missed the extra point. Saints 24, Spartans 20.

I had found in my coaching that sometime during the year a player might come along to be a star, someone unexpected. I shouldn't have worried about the game because unknown to me, Franklin Powell had been harboring a big load of fury the whole evening. We kicked to them and held them at their thirty-five. After we received their punt, Franklin played like he had played in earlier ball games, raging down the field, carrying their big linebackers like they weighed one fifteen instead of two fifteen. Again he ran out the back of their end zone, banging into the fence, getting up stunned but laughing, jumping up and down like a six-year-old in a mud puddle. There's always something intimidating about a back in high school who weighs two forty.

Priest kicked the point and we were finally ahead, 27 to 24, with five minutes left, but we had to kick to them, knowing they had a mountain of talent. We spread our defense, willing to give them five yards but not a touchdown. Just as Franklin had done, they drove relentlessly toward our goal line, mixing passes and runs, and at our eight, they fumbled, we recovered. We were in ecstasy. With three and a half minutes left, our grandstands were a scene of bedlam, my relief bigger than all outdoors. The noise level was a thousand decibels.

We took over and our hero Franklin fumbled it back to them when a linebacker speared the ball. We were in agony. Our demons went after the ball with a fury unmatched the whole frustrating year, and Michler tore the ball away from them. After we had used up the maximum time with Turkey falling on the ball as he took it from the center, Saint Paul used its last time out.

We had the ball on our own five. I brought Turkey over to the bench, telling him, "When you get the ball from center, step back into the end zone and kneel, taking a safety, that'll give them two points but we'll kick to them from the twenty. We'll still be ahead and they shouldn't have time to score again." I don't think Turkey quite understood what I was asking him to do, intentionally giving the other team points, but he did it. It was one of the few times I had used a safety like this in my career, but it was the best thing I did all night. Time ran out, we won 27 to 26 and were headed for the finals of the state championship.

# 27

# STREETS' QUESTIONING

THE POWERFUL, DYNAMIC, TEMPERAMENTAL, unbending Streets Jackson was confused. It was no wonder he wasn't the dynamo in a ball game he had always been. His mother had been terribly hurt in an automobile accident, and because of him, she had gone to the hospital a second time, unconscious, almost dying. It was his fault, God was mad at him and he didn't understand God very well. He couldn't tear through the line or around the ends like he always had because of his confusion. His tremendous physique and coordination could still make him do things he had always done, like scoring the touchdown on the kickoff in the Saint Paul game, but he wasn't fired up every minute.

Streets' mother was much better, her color was good again and she was eating with enthusiasm. Streets and Gertrude sat in their living room with Coach Johnson, talking quietly about football and school, about church and God, about the Jackson family.

"I hear you're studying better, Streets. Am I hearing it right?" Coach Johnson burdened the chair he spoke from.

Ducking his head, slightly embarrassed by his previous poor efforts as a student, Streets grinned. "Yes sir, Coach. I've decided to try harder and see if I can't bring my grades up some. I've sure been a bad example to my brothers and sisters, just trying to get by, and I'm gonna change that."

He paused for a moment, then continued. "Do you think football's wrong, Coach? Maybe God doesn't like the violence."

It was impossible not to be impressed by Coach Johnson. His natural hair was gray around the edges and he had chosen to wear the black minister's shirt with it's white collar. A large silver cross hung from his neck. He effected a small beard, neatly trimmed, also slightly gray. He rumbled, "Son, if I thought God didn't like for us to play football, do you think I'd be involved in it? You're right, it can be rough, and if you play it you can expect to get bloody noses and sprained ankles and knees and sometimes worse, but then all of life is hard and we have to learn to accept what's handed to us. I think football teaches some of that. Do you remember the first time you got a bloody nose and found out it really didn't hurt all that bad? That's one of life's good lessons and we have to learn from it. Now don't get me wrong, I said football was rough, but there's never any excuse for playing dirty. If you're gonna play football, you have to play with all your heart or you're no good, but if you play dirty, you've lost sight of the reason you're playing. It's a game, even if we forget that and give it more importance than it deserves, but people shouldn't get involved in things unless they give their hearts to them."

"What about this church thing, Preacher? You know we've never gone to church before because Momma's too tired and the rest of us jus' don't go."

"First of all, son, don't confuse the church house with God. God is everywhere and the church house is just a building. We need churches 'cause that's where believers go to worship together. God does expect us to worship him, he even tells us to , and y'all have been ignoring Him. God doesn't like to be ignored."

Gertrude looked pained. "Preacher, do you think that's the reason I had that wreck and Henry Junior's had so many problems?" It was the first time the preacher-coach had heard Streets' mother call him by his given name. She had become so used to calling him by the neighborhood name, she rarely used it.

Caleb laughed a little, then looked serious. "No, ma'am. I don't think God works that way, because if he did, things would sure go a lot better. If every time someone did something wrong, God punished him, and every time we did something right, God rewarded us, we sure would be better people. No, I think He mostly lets us stumble along on our own, making our own problems, creating bad or good things around us."

Two of the smaller Jackson girls and Jonathan had come into the room and had taken seats where they could listen. They were in awe of the "Preacher Man" and didn't interrupt the conversation.

"What about us goin' to church, do you think it'll help us any?"

.Caleb's cross swung as he leaned forward, "It always helps, son. You need to read your Bible so you can see what God wants us to do, but he expects us to pay a lot of attention to him, and even though you'll see people at church that you know aren't doing just what He wants, God demands you to worship. It's between you and Him, between each person and Him. And, Henry Junior, if you'd come sit on the front row of the church you'd help me more than you know, and you'd be an example to others."

After Coach Johnson left, Streets decided to talk to Latisha's mother. When he walked up to the Washington's front door, he wondered if Northella would answer his ring. He knew Latisha was working in Lakeland so there wouldn't be any clumsy situation because of her. It was Tuesday evening, practice was over, and the big game wasn't until a week from Friday.

Northella wasn't thrilled. She opened the door about six inches and said in an unkind voice, "What do you want?"

All his life Streets had avoided situations like this, never wanting anyone to humble him, and he felt some of the old anger at someone talking to him like that, but he had to start somewhere. "I'd just like to talk to your for a few minutes, Miz Washington."

"About what?"

"About me, ma'am."

"About you, Streets, I don't want to talk about you."

"I know it, Miz Washington, but I was just hopin' you'd talk to me for a little bit."

Other people might have been cowed by this forbidding athlete, this neighborhood scourge, but Northella Washington wasn't one of them. "What in the world do you and I have to talk about, Streets?"

"It's about me changin' ma'am. I know you've never liked me or approved of me, and I know why. I know I've been a pain in the neck before but I'm tryin' to be different."

"All right, son, come in the house and sit down."

The Washington house was a stinging contrast to what

Streets was used to. Papa Washington had a good job, there was only one child, and Northella was as precise as her daughter. Everything was so neat Streets almost hated to sit down.

"First, Miz Washington, I know you don't like me very much, and I understand it. You know I've always had a chip on my shoulder because it's been tough for us. My momma tries hard but everything's a struggle."

"How is your mother, son?"

"She's doin' pretty good, good enough to go back to work next week."

"Well, that's fine." Northella seemed genuinely concerned and that surprised Streets. "We were all worried about her."

"I appreciate that, Miz Washington. Sometimes I think people don't care about us at all."

"Well, we do. Now I know your family's had it rough, but that's no cause for you to be so mean."

"No ma'am. I guess because I'm strong, I've always felt like I could push people around and that made up for us bein' kind of, of, well, underprivileged." Streets hated to say the words, hated to say anything which demeaned him or his family.

"Well boy," Streets hated the word boy but since he was trying so hard to talk to Northella, he stifled his desire to object, "people don't judge you because you don't have a lot of things, they judge you for what you are." It was a half-truth and they both knew it. "Now, what was it you wanted to talk to me about?"

"About me tryin' to change. I don't know if I can, but I'm goin' to try. I'm not forcin' myself on anyone, not Latisha nor anyone else. I do like her a lot but that's not the reason I came over here. I came because I've always felt like you hated me more than anyone else in the neighborhood and I can't stand it. I just want you to see I'm tryin' to change. I guess that's about it, ma'am."

Latisha's mother had a grim look on her face. "No, son, that's not quite all we need to talk about. You got a baby over in Auburndale. What are you going to do about that?"

Streets looked down at his shoes. "There's nothin' I can do about that, Miz Washington. I can't pay to help take care of it and I sure can't bring it to my house because nobody here could take care of it. The girl's grandmother is takin' care of the baby right now. Maybe in the future I can help support the baby, but I'm helpless to do anything with me still in high school."

Northella's eyes sparked, "You should've thought about that before you started messing around, shouldn't you? Now you see why I'm scared for Latisha to have anything to do with you?"

"Yes ma'am, I do."

After leaving Latisha's house, Streets went to the weight room for thirty minutes, then ran two easy laps around the track, fast enough to do some good, not as blazingly fast as he was capable.

On Wednesday at school, Streets asked Bruce Tucker if he could talk to him during his planning period.

"Sure, Streets. What is it you want to talk to me about?"

It seemed to Streets that he was always having to explain to someone why he wanted to talk to them. "About college, Coach Tucker. I figured you'd have some ideas for me and you're easy to talk to."

Outside it was raining lightly, a gentle fall rain. The temperature hung on a chilly forty-five degrees and there were a few obviously cold students who had on clothes too light for the chill.

Streets said, "I've never really been serious about my school work before and I could always get by, but I've decided if I'm going to college, I better know what I ought to study. I don't even know what it is you study at college."

"Okay, Streets. Let me explain some things to you. First of all, you'll surely get a scholarship for playing football at a major university. A university is made up of many colleges such as the colleges of business, engineering, education, agriculture, and so forth. The first year you'll take general courses which will probably include first year college math, biology, English, history, things like that. You'll choose a major field of study in something you like or feel will be good for a career, but you don't have to do that right at first. Do you have something you'd really like to make your major field?"

"Haven't thought about it, Coach. I always thought I'd play pro football and wouldn't need to worry about the subjects. I figured the coaches would make it easy for me, so I never even thought about it."

Bruce laughed. "Streets you're as green as a gourd, and you'd better be thinking about it. You've got time to think it over. First, you must think about this fact: that only a very small percentage of college athletes are lucky enough and good enough to play pro ball."

"I guess I never knew that. I thought most of them went into the pros."

"I don't know the exact figures, but I'm sure it's only a small percent, probably between one and three percent of college players make the pros. That means only maybe three out of every hundred are good enough to be successful in professional football, so you'd better plan to major in something that leads to a good job. These are tough times, Streets, when good men are being laid off good jobs because the companies can get the work done overseas and pay the workers less. You've got to pick a profession that's in great demand and then get so well qualified and so much better at it than anyone else, that they just have to hire and keep you. Otherwise, you might get a college degree and still not be guaranteed a good job."

Streets looked thoughtful and said, "Great Lord A'mighty, I never knew it was that tough. D'you think I could major in math, Coach?"

Bruce leaned back in his teacher's chair. "Sure you could, but you'd have to change the way you study. Right now you're floating along on your I.Q. I know you've never studied much outside class, and in college a math major has to work very hard. You must understand that an excellent college student studies most of the time he's awake. He has a lot of time between classes when he could goof off in a soda shop or sit on a bench, loafing and watching the girls go by, but where he needs to be is in the library trying to keep up with all his classes. You'll be playing football, so about five months of the year you have to be at football practice about three and a half hours a day. After you have your supper, you have to study until bedtime every day, or else you won't be an excellent student. All the extra time you have on Saturday or Sunday you have to study. It's the hardest thing I know, much harder than digging a ditch. The question is: How much guts, how much character do you have?"

The surroundings had faded from Streets' thoughts as he considered the ideas Bruce was putting in his head. Streets had no conception that college would be that hard. Maybe he ought to consider a major in physical education or recreation that wouldn't be as complicated as math. He didn't see how he could possibly study all that time. Crap! He'd never really studied at all except in the classroom. The athlete rubbed his slightly whiskered chin and shook his head. "I don't know if I want to work that hard."

Coach Tucker took a slide rule from his desk drawer and

moved the slide back and forth unconsciously. "You've had a hard time around here lately, partly because you've thought your ability as an athlete and your superior body put you above other people. The coaches say you're trying to change your attitude and I'm glad your thinking about college because that's where you'll be this time next year. If you'll think back to the time you started playing junior high football and realize how fast the time has gone, college goes just as fast. It's the most important four or five years of your life, so give it a lot of thought, and come back to talk with me some more."

Streets unfolded himself from the student desk and put his hand out to Bruce. "Coach, I thank you. You've been a big help and I'm going to the library to look at some college catalogs."

# 28

# Bruce and Natalie

When Bruce Tucker finished his last class, he wondered what he should do about Natalie and her mother. He had fallen in love with Natalie and wanted to marry her, but her mother stood between them like the Rock of Gibraltar. He couldn't very well take Natalie's mother into his home because surely the children would be a bone of contention. A dinosaur bone. The kids liked Natalie, and though it would be tough for all of them to get used to each other, he thought the children and Natalie could adjust. In case of any difficulty, he would always be in the middle. But Natalie's mother was a different proposition. She had only her husband's social security pension and probably wouldn't consider looking for a job because she'd never worked outside the home. Natalie and he would have to provide for her. First, though, he'd have to find out if Natalie would marry him, and if she would, they could present the wonderful idea to the selfish old biddy. Oops, he ought to try not to think that way.

When Natalie and Bruce arrived at their favorite dining place on Wednesday night, they were happy with each other. Bruce could tell from her conversation and from her attitude toward him, that it was a very good time in her life. When they were seated at the secluded table, he took Natalie's hand. "Do you know that I love you, precious woman?"

She gasped, leaning toward him. "Oh, Bruce, you've made me so happy with everything you say and do, and you must know I love you too. I'm almost scared to even say it because it seems too good to be true. This time last year I was floundering up there in Ohio, not even knowing you existed. I was lonely but hardly thinking about it, and now you've come into my life. If I were any happier, I couldn't stand it." She squeezed his hand and realized he was squeezing hers so hard it hurt.

Bruce stood, walked the two steps to her side of the table and in spite of the two other tables of diners in their area, he took Natalie into his arms and kissed her as if there were no one else present. There was some giggling form the other tables, then a little applause. They sat down, blushing, but glowing with their love.

"Will you marry me, my darling?"

"Bruce, you're a smart man, and that's a stupid question. Of course I'll marry you. In fact, if you don't marry me, I'm going to haunt you. I love you so much."

They finished their meal, though neither could have said what they ate. On the way home, they parked on the shore of one of the hundreds of lakes which dot Florida's ridge section. After a period of kissing and hugging which became ever more heated, Natalie said, "We'd really better get married, because I see where this is going."

Bruce laughed. "You're right, that's exactly where it's going."

When she reached home, Natalie went straight to her room, not wanting to spoil the evening with a family discussion.

After an almost sleepless night, and a day when she floated through her classes, Natalie was at home with her mother after school. "Mother, I have something I want to tell you and I hope you won't get mad."

Amanda Shires glared at her daughter. Apparently, she could think of nothing Natalie could tell her that required an introduction, that wouldn't irritate her. "Well, I'm sure it's not good news, but go ahead."

"Bruce and I want to get married."

"Married!" Amanda jumped out of her chair and screamed the words so loudly that Natalie knew the neighbors several mobile homes away could hear her.

"Married!" she screamed again. "No, by God, you're not getting married." Natalie had very rarely heard her mother curse, but apparently it wasn't because she didn't know the words.

"I knew from the first that that evil man was bad for you and this would come to no good end. You're not going to marry anybody," she shouted, "much less an old man with a bunch of children. No, by God, no! You're not going to marry and leave me here to fend for myself, a helpless old lady with no means of support." At a thousand decibels, Amanda continued her tirade. "I knew it from the first, that man just wanted to get in your britches and now he prob'ly has. Married! I hate the word! And you can just forget it because you're not getting married to him or to anyone else, you hear me?"

By this time Natalie was crying, seated on the sofa, her body wrung with great racking sobs.

Natalie looked at her mother, standing in the center of the living room, knees slightly bent, hair a little wild, eyes continuing to send out flashes of light with each screamed invective. Again she thought WITCH. This time the younger woman was not so quick to withdraw that opinion of her mother. Natalie knew she had made every effort for years to make life nice for her mother. Perhaps that was the problem. Amanda Shires had lived on the edge of luxury for many years, her every reasonable comfort taken care of by a dutiful daughter, and the girl knew her mother reveled in it. Natalie had never minded furnishing most of her mother's support. Her father's social security check certainly helped, but the main support came from Natalie. Mama knew it too. She wasn't about to let the good life walk out the front door, or so she thought.

It was a sparkling day outside. There had been no bitter frost to kill off the multicolored crotons and they were beautiful. Yesterday's front had passed and the blue sky smiled down on the palm tree-lined streets. Most mobile homes had citrus trees, the orange and yellow fruit was obvious amid the deep green of the leaves. All of this escaped the attention of Natalie and her mother, lost in the emotion of the moment.

Several neighbors stood in the street, looking toward the home from which the screams and crying were coming.

Natalie looked up from her crying, eyes red and face pinched with the torture of the moment. "Mother, I wouldn't take away my support of you, but I have a right to my own life, too. This may be my only chance to marry a good man, and you're not going to stop it."

Amanda Shires had tears in her eyes, too. "Where will I

live? I can't support myself here, Natalie. Ooooh, you're such a mean, mean girl, to think of leaving a poor helpless old lady alone to fend for herself. Remember all the years I've supported you in my house and never complained. I certainly wouldn't go live with that evil man you're thinking of marrying." Amanda sat in one of the chairs and started to moan. "I'd be nothing but a baby sitter." First it was just a little moan, but it grew louder and more strident until Natalie knew they could hear it at the recreation complex two blocks away.

There was a knock on the door of the screen porch. The younger woman went to answer it, to be greeted by a bulky woman with a peasant's face, red with blotches from carelessness in the tropical sunshine. "Is everything all right in there? Do you need some help?"

Disheveled and teary eyed, Natalie told her, "Everything's all right, we're just having a misunderstanding." Natalie knew it didn't sound like a misunderstanding but she hated to tell the neighbors all the grisly details.

From inside, the combative Amanda Shires screamed out, "Mind your own business, you nosy old biddy."

Embarrassed to further tears, Natalie returned to the scene of combat. She went directly to her room, took a suitcase off the closet shelf and started to throw clothes in it haphazardly. Her mother followed her into the room, asking, "What are you doing, Natalie? You can't do this. After all the things I've done for you all your life, you can't walk out on me. You're not going to marry that man, do you hear me. He's bad, Natalie, can't you see that. I could tell from the look in his eyes, from the way he walked and talked, you ungrateful girl. I was afraid it might come to this." As she spoke, the wild-eyed older woman placed herself squarely in the doorway to prevent Natalie from leaving the room. "You're not leaving, do you hear?" Natalie shouldered her way past her mother, the fire of the moment giving her strength she seldom possessed and the unreasonableness of her mother making her so mad she almost could not think.

"Where are you going? What am I going to do?"

Natalie was by now so mad, she really didn't care what her mother did. "Just do what you've been doing, live off the fat of the land, sit your fat ass down in that kitchen and stuff yourself like you usually do. You'll get by just like you always have, and the world can bet it won't be because you work for what you get! Natalie hated to be reduced to cursing, but at this point she was beyond concern.

Natalie walked out the front door, slamming it behind her, throwing her one suitcase in the back seat of the car. She backed out of the driveway, burnt rubber when she left the front, and drove recklessly out the exit from the park. She didn't know where she was going, she just had to get out of the presence of her mother. She drove around for an hour, then went to a motel in Winter Haven. It was a miserable time, but she needed time to think for herself.

Natalie turned the television on and quickly realized she was in no condition to watch it. She locked the door, walked to the lobby of the motel and bought a newspaper. When she returned to her room she was as unsuccessful at reading the newspaper as she had been at watching television. She tried to grade a stack of homework papers from school and found that more difficult than reading the newspaper. She burst into tears, sat on the bed and let the crying wash over her. After a few minutes of crying, she wiped her eyes and called Bruce.

When he answered the phone, Bruce could tell Natalie had been crying. "What's the matter, honey?"

"Well, I told my mother we were going to get married and she didn't take it very well." She emitted another racking sob.

"Yeah, I gather that from your condition. Where are you?"

Natalie sobbed, "I'm in Winter Haven at the Snowbird Motel. I couldn't stay with mother another minute. Can you come see me?"

"I think so, Natalie, but I'll have to see if I can get someone to stay with the kids. Give me your phone number and I'll call you back in a few minutes."

When Bruce showed up at the motel forty-five minutes later, she greeted him with a sob and with an engulfing kiss. When they separated, he said, "Wow!"

They sat on the bed while Natalie told Bruce of the scene at her mobile home. "It was awful, Bruce. I knew it would be bad but I didn't think it would be that bad. We threw a scene for the neighbors they won't soon forget." With that statement, Natalie giggled and then burst into another long sob.

Bruce had his arm around Natalie and drew her closer. He kissed her again and, with passion born of frustration and longing, she became lost in the embrace. They lay back on the bed and continued to kiss passionately. He started to unbutton her blouse and she sat up.

"I can't do that yet, Bruce. I'm not rejecting you. I love you and want you so much, but all of my years of not doing it are because it's not what we're supposed to do. I'll marry you as soon as you want, but please, let's wait until then."

The room with its blue motif was modest but nice, though neither of them would have cared if it were a luxury suite or a hovel. It had the usual television set, king size bed, dresser and chest of drawers, closet, lavatory area, and separate bath. A print of an Audubon pelican looked down from the wall behind the bed, and a large summer scene from the everglades occupied a prominent place on the largest wall space.

Bruce said, "You've got to marry me soon. I can't stand to want you so bad much longer."

"Oh, Bruce," she said as she kissed him again. "I've never had anybody in my whole life and I have so much to give. You're so perfect for me and I never dreamed I could be so lucky as to find you. You can't know what it's like to be over thirty and still be a virgin. Please, let's get married right away."

In order not to test their willpower more, they went to a movie. It was much like trying to read the newspaper, neither of them could get interested in what was playing.

After Bruce left, Natalie thought of calling her mother, then decided against it, hoping her mother was as miserable as she was. She turned the television on and pretended to watch, having little success. At one o'clock she turned off the light but never closed her eyes. She arose at five, dressed for school, and ate a danish in the motel dining room. She had two strong cups of coffee, hoping it would fortify her for the day.

At seven o'clock she called her mother. Amanda sounded frantic when she answered the phone. "Where are you, Natalie, and how could you do this to me? I've worried the whole night long, not knowing where you were, you thoughtless girl."

"I'm all right, Mother. I will be at school as usual today, and I'll come home after school to talk to you." Natalie hung up the phone, satisfied that she was doing the right thing.

When Bruce came to her room after school, he said, "When, Natalie, are we going to get married?"

"As soon as you want, Bruce. I'm past ready."

At home, Natalie asked her mother to sit down at the

breakfast nook. She said, "Mother, Bruce and I are going to be married very soon. I love him and he is so right for me, I can't believe it. You were married and I have a right to marriage, too. I'll support you but I don't want to hear any more about it.

They both ignored the beauty of their surroundings. The rules of the Lake Honey Mobile Home Park were strict and the homes were neat, the lawns manicured, the vegetation beautiful. None of this mattered in the emotion of the moment.

Amanda said, "You're such an ungrateful child, after all I've done for you all your life. I told you, I'm not going to go live with that sorry man you're marrying."

"You've got that right, Mother, you're not going to live with us." Natalie stood up from the breakfast nook. "You've become a selfish woman, used to having your own way, and you'd not be fit company for anyone. You've bossed me around for years, and thank heavens I don't have to take it anymore. I'll support you here and you can be as selfish as you want on your own."

# 29

# Saturday Six Days to Game Time

ON SATURDAY MORNING, STREETS AWOKE AT five o'clock. His first thought on opening his eyes was six days until the big game. He knew everyone on the team and all the coaches were thinking the same thing. It was on their minds every minute of the day, an obsession clinging to them, an all-encompassing presence that occupied not only the team but hundreds in the town who were caught up in it.

Streets was pounded from many directions this dark morning. He was still terribly concerned about his mother's health. Thank God she was recovering and seemed almost well. God had really answered his prayers and the prayers of others he hadn't realized cared about his mother, and he was humbled by the thought. The contempt of the community for his meanness rubbed at him and made him thoughtful. He had thought he could bully people, overpower the weak, earn the admiration of the strong, make love to the broads who were fascinated by him, and do enough work to get by at school.

He had found the coaches tougher than he had thought when he told them they couldn't get along without him. The team members had almost told him to get lost when he turned his back on them. Northella Washington had stood up to him and, in no uncertain terms, had told him what the community thought of him. He had a baby he couldn't support over in the next town, and for the first time, he felt responsible for the child. He knew he couldn't do anything for it without giving up the idea of going to college, and he couldn't do that.

He was back on the football team, but there was an undercurrent, a feeling emanating from the team and from within himself, that he wasn't quite one of them. His play had been spotty. If he were another player and not Streets Jackson, they would have thought he was good. With his talent and the brilliant plays he had made in previous games, his recent efforts looked mediocre. Powell was still running first-string tailback and that ate at Streets like a rasp. He was still trying to understand the part that God should play in his life and it was confusing. God had answered his prayers and Streets felt obligated to Him for that. He thought he might start going to listen to Coach Johnson down at the church house and see if it made more sense to him. The coach was giving his love and concern to the community for some reason Streets didn't quite understand.

What Northella Washington had said to him rankled him, but it made him thoughtful and he could see why Northella didn't want Latisha going with him.

He had been really working at school, the last couple of tests he had taken were easier, he had made better grades than before and he liked the feeling. He was working on his homework at night, and having seen his big brother studying had made Jonathan spend time at the dinner table with his books, too. Once before a teacher had said to him, "Streets, why don't you study more? You could really be an example for others."

He had quickly replied. "Don't make me no example. I don't want to be a leader that way."

On this Saturday morning, as he threw the quilt aside, Streets poked Jonathan and said, "Okay, John-John, let's rise and shine, we've got a lot of fruit to snatch off those trees this mornin'."

The boy groaned and in a sleepy voice said, "You go ahead Streets, I'll git up in a minute."

Streets laughed and pulled the quilt off the bed, leaving Jonathan without any cover. "You ain't goin' to pull that on me this mornin', brother, we gotta make some money and we won't have no better chance than today."

The older boy reached down and pulled Jonathan's legs around and placed his feet on the floor. He sat there, head resting on his hands as he tried to wake up. Streets stood his younger brother on his feet and handed him his trousers. Jonathan laughed and said, "Brother, you don't let up, do you?"

In the kitchen, Streets took six eggs out of the refrigerator and broke them into a dish, added a little milk and stirred them, then put them into the frying pan. He took out eight slices of bread, put two in the toaster, and pushed the lever down. He didn't bother with juice because he knew when they were in the grove, they would eat two or three oranges. He heated the water for some grits and put the oleo on the table. In ten minutes their breakfast was ready.

His mother slept soundly on the couch and for this, Streets was grateful. The last few days she had begun to look rested and well, and was supposed to return to work on Monday morning. Some sounds came from the neighborhood as it began to awaken to a busy Saturday morning. People on their way to work, babies crying for their morning milk, the coughing of the cigarette smokers, the sounds of the automobile engines starting, none of these were shielded by the uninsulated walls of the Jackson home.

It was chilly this November morning and both Streets and Jonathan wore denim jackets. They caught the yellow bus which had been retired by the county school board, with an undecipherable number of miles on the odometer. It was a sixteen mile ride to the grove this morning, and there was some easy banter from the men who made up the crew.

"Are y'all goin' to win that ball game this week, Streets?"

"Sure we are," the big athlete answered. He couldn't very well say they weren't going to win and he felt they would.

"What kind of a team is it, Streets, how'd they git into the playoffs?"

Streets leaned forward, resting his head on his hands on the metal rail above the seat, and said, "I figure if a team is good enough to get into the finals, they must do about everything right. You've gotta have a good kicking game and good coaching, good runners and good passing. Daytona Inland has all of these things, but if you're lookin' for one thing they do better than anything else, it's prob'ly their runnin' game."

The bus rumbled south on highway 27, a road already busy with the traffic caused by the citrus industry.

Streets continued his description of the Daytona team. "If you're lookin' for one thing that team does better than most other teams, it's probably the two runnin' backs they have, named Black and White. The funny thing is, the one named Black is a white boy, and the one named White is black." At this, the men on the bus exploded with laughter. Streets spoke again, "They're both fast as greased lightin' and very shifty, so they've both scored a lot of touchdowns. Also they're the best of friends and are always together and that's made the team work together real well. Beatin' them is goin' to be tough to do."

When they arrived at the grove, they found the trees were about fifteen years old and would be good picking. The trees were close together, which meant more profit per acre for the grove owner.

They had been picking for about an hour when one of the pickers screamed and jumped off his ladder. He yelled, "Great God Almighty, I want you to look at this." All the crew came running, looking up into the tree where the man was pointing. There was a huge diamondback rattlesnake, draped around one of the limbs, partly hidden by the thick foliage. It was a danger they always faced, as many pickers had been killed over the years by rattlesnakes in the trees. Someone went to the bus, got a shovel, knocked the snake out of the tree, and killed it. It measured five foot two inches and looked as deadly as it was.

By noon Streets and Jonathan had picked eight big bins of oranges between them. Before the day was over, they had earned over one hundred sixty dollars.

# Sunday Five Days to Game Time

When Streets walked the four blocks to Caleb Johnson's church with his family on Sunday morning, he knew his mother was proud. All her children were dressed in their best clothes and looked good. The handsome Streets and his sixteen-year-old brother would have looked good to any young lady, and Streets' virility was already a caution flag to many a mother.

When they lined up near the back, they filled the whole row. Caleb came to each of them and shook their hands. He was dressed in a big black robe with a large silver cross suspended from his neck, and looking at him, some of his parishioners felt he could have rolled back the Red Sea without any help from Moses.

All the brothers rushed to shake hands with Streets and he didn't much like it. He was curious about the place of God in his life, but he didn't know if he could stand all this brotherhood stuff. He'd sure have to talk to Coach Johnson about that.

In his sermon, Caleb used the scripture about the talents and Streets was pleased when Caleb read about some men having five talents, some having two talents, some having one talent. He knew he was one of those with the five talents. When Caleb put a different slant on it, and said God expected people to use what He had given them for God's own good, that made it a lot harder sermon for Streets. He had a lot of talking to do with the preacher man.

Gertrude Jackson had left a meatloaf and potatoes in the oven, and beans in the crock pot. The girls set the table and it took only a few minutes for Gertrude to put the dinner on. Much of the conversation at the table was about church, some about the coming Friday night's ball game, and some about Mother going back to work.

Streets read the Lakeland Ledger, looking over the sports page with its attention to the Citrus-Inland state finals game. Inland was favored by eight points as they were unbeaten and it looked like it would be a fight to the finish. Streets didn't much mind Inland being favored, it kinda took the pressure off. He knew how powerful Citrus City was, how much talent the team had, and it didn't worry him that Inland was favored. He said to himself, "It'll take a damn good, I mean darn good team to beat us."

He knew the coaches were at Coach Warren's house reviewing two of the Inland game films and going over the scouting report. He called Coach Warren and asked if he could watch the films. "Sure, Streets, come on over, maybe you'll see some weakness we don't see."

Playing in the defensive backfield had been good for the big athlete. It had made him much more conscious of the way the plays developed, and he liked to watch the pass patterns of the opponents. As he observed the Inland film, Streets thought the potential pass receivers were sometimes careless with their patterns, not making sharp enough cuts, or telegraphing their intentions. Other than that, he could see no weaknesses.

Black and white looked as good in the films as they were played up in the newspapers. Each was about five eight and weighed less than one hundred seventy pounds. They were very shifty and the Daytona Beach News Journal sportswriters often referred to them as the twins. It brought laughter from some readers, and Black and White enjoyed it. Their parents had begun to sit together at the games, making a good feeling among the spectators.

Streets decided it would take a masterful performance by the Citrus City team to win on Friday.

After leaving the coaches' meeting, Streets went home and slept for two hours, waking up hungry and feeling strong. He often slept on Sunday afternoon, figuring it renewed his already strong body. He ate more of the meatloaf dinner, then went to the church house and listened to Caleb Johnson's sermon. Every sermon made Streets think Caleb had prepared it specifically for him, then he laughed at his reaction, knowing it was his conscience that made him feel that way.

When he went home, he worked on his math and English for two and a half hours with Jonathan at his side.

It was a very satisfying Sunday and Streets felt happier than he had in a long time.

# 31

# Monday Four Days to Game Time

**M**onday was a disaster, a day which should never have happened. When Streets arrived on the campus, his first sight was Hunky King on crutches. Four days to kickoff and one of the best football players in Florida on crutches.

Streets asked his friend, "What happened, man?"

Hunky, obviously distressed, said, "I don't really know, Streets. I started walkin' down the steps at my house and all of a sudden it hurt in the back of my knee. In about an hour, I couldn't put any weight on it at all, so I went to the doctor."

"Did he think you'd be able to play this week? Man, we' got to have you."

"The doc said I'd be awful lucky if this thing improved enough by Friday night to be able to play. He gave me some medicine, and I'll be in the whirlpool every day, and movin' the leg as much as I can, but he said we'd just have to wait and see."

It was a gray day, with a lingering fog and some smoke from long-smoldering muck fires hanging low over the campus. The foliage had surrendered some of its color to the melancholy of the day, and people were quieter than usual as the sullen day took away some of their vigor. Between classes, as the students moved along the covered walkways to change classes, a fight broke out between a black and a white student. A big crowd gathered immediately and it had to be broken up by Caleb Johnson. There had been no major racial incidents at Citrus City High School, in contrast to other schools where there had been huge problems. The rest of the day the tension was almost unbearable.

Streets found it hard to concentrate in the classroom. His mind kept turning to Hunky King's ailing leg, thinking about his mother back at work for the first time, about college next year, about his reputation with Latisha Washington's mother and others in the community. When his English teacher called on him, he was in another world and had to ask that the question be repeated.

Obviously irritated, the teacher asked, "Have you read any of the novels on the list I gave you?"

"No, ma'am I guess I haven't."

When the teacher said, "Well, I suggest you do, because half your grade this six weeks depends on your knowledge of those novels. I know you think you're a privilege character, but that doesn't go in here."

Streets' temper, never very far hidden below the surface, reached its familiar boiling point, and he rose and walked out of the room. As he reached the door, he said to himself, "Who the hell does she think she is, talking to me like that." He knew he'd been trying hard and it irritated him to think his good efforts weren't noticed. He hadn't read any of the novels, but he'd been busy with so many things, he hadn't had time. He sat on a bench outside the gym until the period was over.

When Streets was settled in Bruce Tucker's class, the public address system blared, "Streets Jackson, please report to the office."

At the office, Streets met a highly irritated English teacher, Mrs. Thornton, and principal Oscar Seidthorn. Mrs. Thornton jumped on the complaint with both high heels. "This student is not doing his work in my class, and when I reprimanded him, he jumped up like a jack in the box and ran out of my room. He thinks he can have his way wherever he is." The tall, gaunt teacher, divorced and unhappy, apparently enjoyed finding some student to punish for a real or imagined fault. Her dyed black hair, pulled back severely into a bun, glistened in the glare of the fluorescent light.

Mrs. Thornton wasn't the only one who was irritated, Streets also had a full head of stream. He knew how to get some advantage in the situation. "She called me a privilege character, and teachers have no business calling students names, and she did it because I'm black."

Oscar Seidthorn was afraid of Streets,. He didn't want to make the muscular athlete mad at him, and although he wanted to mollify the teacher, he knew this was not the week to make the whole town furious with him by interfering with Streets' normal schedule. He must play in the game on Friday night. The principal told the irate teacher, "Leave this problem with me, Mrs. Thornton. I'll take care of it."

When the teacher had returned to her classroom, Mr. Seidthorn asked Streets, "Now, what's this all about?"

Streets laid out the facts for the principal. Then he added, "I've been tryin' real hard, Mr. Seidthorn. She just caught me when my mind was on somethin' else and then she insulted me. I know I need to read those books and I will, but she's got no business calling me names."

Compared to the fight which had occurred this morning, this was an insignificant problem. He had a frustrated teacher and a student-athlete who had strutted around like a peacock as long has he had known him, but this was easily solved. Mrs. Thornton would settle down, and it was very important that Streets not be interfered with.

"Streets, I can't see that you've done much of anything wrong except to leave that lady's class without permission, but you've got some things to learn. One is that you can make people a lot happier if you'll butter them up a little and I think you need to do that with Mrs. Thornton. If you'll apologize to her, whether you want to or not, tell her some of the things you've been going through lately, you'll probably have a friend rather than an enemy. Remember, you have to take that English grade with you to college next year and you sure don't want to have that lady for an enemy. I don't blame you if she irritates you, sometimes she irritates me, too." Streets had to laugh at what Mr. Seidthorn said; he'd never viewed the principal as simply a human being before.

It made good sense to Streets. He thanked Mr. Seidthorn and went back to Bruce Tucker's class. After school, Streets walked back to Mrs. Thornton's room to find the sour looking lady bent purposely over some papers, slapping red marks on them like a painter on a canvas. He hesitated to spoil her fun.

"Mrs. Thornton, may I interrupt you?"

"All right, young man, you may, but make it brief because you can see I'm terribly busy."

Streets was uncomfortable apologizing to anyone for anything. He felt like he had been wronged and it was a new experience for him to try to smooth things over; that was other peoples' responsibility rather than his. In this unique situation he said, "Mrs. Thornton, I'm sorry I wasn't paying attention when you called on me today. I've had so many things on my mind lately, it's hard to concentrate. My mother's been in the hospital twice lately, and she could have died. My daddy died in a wreck several years ago, and I've been responsible for my seven brothers and sisters since my mother was hurt. Also, there's been some trouble between me and Coach Warren and we've about got that straightened out. Still, it worries me. I've been tryin' harder on my assignments than I used to, so I'll be sure to read those books. I'm sorry I made it difficult for you."

The starchy lady, surprised by Streets' apology, was thoughtful. She'd never been to a Citrus City athletic event, being as interested in athletics as she was in ancient Mongolian history. She was only aware of Jackson's prowess because of the press she couldn't help but notice, and because the other students seemed to be so wary of him. Streets' mother's condition was news to her.

She pushed the papers to the side, looking up at Streets.

"I didn't know about your mother, son, and I'm sorry. It must have been a very trying time for you. I hope your mother's much better."

"She is, ma'am, she started back to work today."

As Streets stood before her, arms crossed with bulging muscles pushing on his shirt sleeves, broad-shouldered and handsome, the six foot man must have made her wish she was going home to someone as appealing. She was obviously impressed by his apology and his physical nearness. She actually smiled. "Well, young man, I'm glad you came back in so we could talk this over. Please read those books soon. You'll like them."

It was drizzling rain as the players milled in the dressing rooms and the coaches wished it would go away. We didn't need any sick players so we hesitated to go outside, but we needed the practice. When the drizzle let up, the team ran to the practice field behind the stadium, went through calisthenics, then separated for offensive and defensive drills. Occasionally, a team can be either very impressive in practice, or very sloppy, and this was, for some unknown reason, one of the sloppy days. The offense missed handoffs, dropped passes, and generally messed up. It was really gloomy Monday. When a terrible bolt of lightning hit the middle of the nearby lake, I told the team to head for the gym.

Inside the gym, we went over the scouting report again, bringing out points we might have missed the previous week. We placed the team in offensive and defensive positions and walked through plays, showing what might be expected of Daytona Beach Inland. We emphasized the positions occupied by Black and White, Daytona's speedy backs, showing their favorite running plays, then going through Inland passes which were on the films. Still, it was an unsatisfactory practice, leaving both the players and the coaches frustrated.

When Streets reached home, he found his mother lying on the couch, weakened by her first day back at work. She looked pale and it worried the children. He had the girls start supper, then sat with his mother, telling her the events of the day. When Streets told her of his run in with Mrs. Thornton, she shook her head. "Now you be nice to that teacher, son, you need to git a good grade from her."

"I know it Momma, she jus' caught me at a bad time. I talked it over with her after school and I think it's okay now."

After a supper of cornbread, black beans, rice and onions, the youngest children wanted to go outside and play under the streetlight with others from the neighborhood but Streets wouldn't hear of it. "Y'all git your books and sit around that table and work on your school work. We're not goin' to be a family that comes home with bad grades." They did as they were told, not wanting any of Streets' well-known temper to crash down on their heads. He could get their attention.

# 32

# Tuesday Three Days to Game Time

As Streets walked the eight blocks to school, he passed Northella Washington who was going the opposite way. She waved to him and he nearly fainted. He laughed aloud, saying to himself, "Imagine that, Latisha's mother waving at me." He jumped up, clicking his heels, drawing laughter from an elderly couple who sat on their porch nearby.

A block later, Alfonius Jefferson joined him and immediately jumped into the subject which had polarized the campus on the previous day. "What'd you think of that fight yesterday, Streets?"

Streets' Monday had been too full of other things for him to be interested in the fight. He had heard about it and knew both participants. Ordinarily, he would have thrown himself into the middle of it, but was struck with a sudden surge of maturity. "I don't know anything about it but rumors, and it looks like an unnecessary argument between a stupid white boy and a stupid black boy, so I'm not goin' to get involved in it."

Alfonius laughed. "I guess you' right, Streets. I hadn't thought about it that way. They're both stupid. How 'bout Hunky, you think he'll be ready to play Friday?"

"Man, I hope so. There's nobody we need worse than we need the Hunk. I guess the doc told him he might be able to play, and I know he got a shot of cortisone yesterday afternoon, so maybe he'll be ready."

As they passed the faculty parking lot, the two football players saw Bruce Tucker talking to Natalie Shires through her open car window.

In the car, Natalie told Bruce, "It was horrible, Bruce. I've never had any trouble with my mother before, but she's so unreasonable I can't understand it. I guess it's such a threat to her, the idea of my moving out and her not having control of me any longer. I must do something because I can't stand to go on like this." Bruce leaned against the window, listening to the woman who had become so dear to him. Along the road nearby, students were walking along in small groups. Across the street from the school a faction was gathered under a spreading live oak tree, smoking a last cigarette before they entered the no smoking zone on the school grounds. Yesterday's front had cleaned the air, moving south to give the burgeoning east coast, the Everglades and Miami a rainy day like central Florida had on Monday.

Bruce, caught up in the emotion of the moment, was oblivious to the students. "Why don't we go to Tampa this afternoon and get a marriage license? That way the locals won't see our application in the paper and we won't draw any more curiosity than we can help."

Natalie was thrilled. "Wonderful, Bruce, wonderful! It'll make me so happy if we do that. Honestly, I want to marry you so much that I can't sleep at night for thinking about it." She took his hand through the window and kissed it. A couple of passing girls saw what happened, pointed and giggled. The romance was about as secret as the oranges on the nearby trees.

When Streets walked into Mrs. Thornton's class, she smiled at him. Another miracle. He took his seat alongside Horst Michler and the two talked briefly about Hunky's bad knee. When Mrs. Thornton rapped her pencil on the desk, the room quieted. The first thing she did was ask Streets whether he had checked out any of the novels from the library.

"Yes ma'am. I decided it might be wise if I did that." What he said drew a huge laugh form the class and even the teacher joined in.

"You seem to have gained some wisdom overnight, young man. Whatever prompted you to do it?" Again, there was laughter, an unaccustomed change in the English class.

Streets was enjoying the repartee. "It just seemed like the right thing to do at the time. I checked out "On the Beach", by Nevil Shute. I read a few chapters and it looks like it might not end happily ever after."

Mrs. Thornton became very serious, "It's a most intriguing and thought-provoking book, Mr. Jackson. I'm glad you've chosen to read that one, though it won't make you happy and it might make you uneasy. We'll discuss it one day soon. You'll find Nevil Shute to write in a manner some of you will think stilted, but he's an Englishman who used the English language brilliantly."

When he went to Bruce Tucker's mathematics class, Streets thought Coach Tucker seemed absorbed in some subject other than the lesson he was teaching. Streets observed that most people were tied up in their own lives, everyone having a different problem. He wondered if Coach Warren was worrying about some problem beside winning this week's football game.

At football practice that afternoon, the coaches spent a lot of time on the kicking game, especially protecting the punter and the extra point man. They tried to practice it nearly every day, and it had paid off. They had no punts blocked, though their kickers had missed several extra points.

An article about the approaching game appeared that day in the Orlando Sentinel, titled "What's Wrong At Citrus City?"

The sportswriter stated:

> There seems to be a problem forty miles south of here with the Citrus City football team. The Spartans played brilliantly during the early part of the season, but they've looked like anything but a state contender in the last few games. We know there has been a problem with the explosive Streets Jackson, but our staff has not been able to learn the particulars from the Citrus City coaches. Other coaches in the same district say that Jackson is egotistical and temperamental and has upset the rhythm of the team. Jackson apparently was disciplined and missed several games for the Spartans, his place being taken by a two hundred forty pound runner named Franklin Powell. Powell has played well, sometimes blasting his way through the opponents, carrying the Spartans to victory.

> Jackson, playing in his regular spot on defense, is effective as always. He has appeared only part-time on offense. In our sports department, we think it shows questionable judgment to hold the fastest player in the state out of the lineup on offense. We think questionable judgment sounds better than dumb. In a phone conversation with Coach Angus Warren, we have learned that Hunky King, one of Citrus City's finest athletes, may not play in Friday's state championship game. At this point, with Citrus City stumbling occasionally, just barely making it into the finals, we have to favor Daytona Inland by two touchdowns.

When he read the Orlando Sentinel account, Streets was embarrassed and irate. He couldn't escape the self-absorption which he had lived with for years and the old temper boiled in him. His first thought was, "Sonsabitches." After supper, he couldn't study because he was so upset by the newspaper article, so he walked to Hunky King's house to discuss the account with him.

He found Hunky in his living room, leg propped in a chair, crutches lying beside him, typing a book report. Streets said, "Hunk, what'd you think of the thing in the Sentinel about our team?"

Hunky laughed, "Man, you' not worried about that thing are you? They've got to write somethin' and this week they have to play up the championship game. Everybody's mind is on it and the sports departments all over the state are full of all the games from all the classifications. We're close to Orlando, so they're more interested in our game than they are the ones from Pensacola and Miami."

"But why'd they have to put that thing in there about me? I haven't had any run in with those reporters." Streets was too upset to see the article with any objectivity.

"It goes with the territory, Streets. You were off the football team for a while and you're one of ten or so athletes the whole state is watching. You're goin' to be in the newspaper whether you want to or not. You haven't been scoring like you were the first part of the season when you were leading in scoring. The whole state is watching you like a hawk."

Streets looked at his good friend, hoping he would be ready to play on Friday night. Hunky was one of the Citrus City athletes who would be receiving many scholarship offers from colleges. He had gained weight as he was maturing, was up to one ninety, built like Atlas, and was one of the super-fast Spartans. Though it was cool outside, the house was warm and the Hunk was dressed in a tee shirt and shorts which showed off his muscles, pumped up by the weight room.

"Is that shot of cortisone doin' you any good, and are you goin' to be ready to play on Friday? We' got to have you."

A worried look crossed King's face. "I don't know, Streets. The knee feels better and I can put some weight on it. Here we are approachin' the game we've worked toward for at least six years and this it he first time I've ever been questionable to start a ball game."

Streets sat on an ottoman, hands clasped around one of his knees, facing King. "I guess it's not hard to see why Daytona might be favored over us, with our problems. I hope Inland is havin' as much trouble as we are."

Hunky changed the subject. "I heard you' been in to talk to Coach Tucker about college. What'd he have to say?"

In the comfortable room, Streets felt welcomed and relaxed. "He told me what to expect the first year of school and how to go about findin' exactly what universities required from a freshman. I sat in the library and went over the catalogs, looked at the courses we'd have to take, and what electives we're allowed the first year."

A visitor unfamiliar with the two young men would be in awe of their physical presence. Each of the football players was handsome; Streets was taller with longer muscles, Hunky more nearly fit the pattern of a weightlifting model but his muscles were not exaggerated. Their conversation, muted by their soft southern accents, was intelligent.

Hunky said, "I hear Bruce Tucker has a real romance goin' with that new teacher from Ohio. A couple of the girls told me they were havin' a serious conversation in the parking lot this morning and she kissed his hand, lookin' like she was really in love with him."

"Yeah, I heard that too. People been seein' them around a lot lately. I expect Mr. Tucker is glad to have a woman back in his life after losin' his wife a few years ago. I like the man, he's one super good teacher and I've felt sorry for him ever since his wife died."

In Hillsborough County, Bruce Tucker and Natalie Shires had been to the courthouse and had completed the necessary papers to obtain their marriage license. They emerged with a sense of contentment, happy with each other. They drove to the old Cuban section of Tampa called Ybor City and ate at one of the well-known restaurants that drew tourists to the area. Natalie felt her life was just starting. A tall, silver-haired, smooth looking major-domo, probably the owner, was greeting the customers, talking in Spanish to some of them, obviously full of his own importance, king of his castle.

In the soft, candlelit atmosphere, Bruce held Natalie's hand. "Do you know how much I love you, pretty girl, and how glad I am that you've come into my life?" He hesitated, then added, "I was really at a loss until the night I sat with you at the coaches' party. You've filled a void in my life, and I love everything about you. The coaches have been telling me how great you are, pretty and sweet and kind, and Caleb Johnson is impressed with you." Bruce stirred his coffee and looked thoughtful. "If Caleb admires you, that's really good because he's a fine judge of character. You're smart, though you try not to overpower people with it. Your figure is terrific, and we'll learn more about that later." Natalie laughed when he said it.

The orchestra played Spanish music in the background, providing a different atmosphere for the two anglos. Squeezing his hand, she answered, "Bruce, darling, I've never loved anyone deeply before, and it's a wonderful experience. I can't get you off my mind, whether I'm in my classroom or home in bed. I have to pinch myself to be sure I'm awake, and when I wake up at home, I'm so thrilled to realize it's really true, that I have you, and that you love me. I love your children and think you've done such a great job with them. I hope they can learn to love me. I'm not Evelyn and won't ever try to take her place in their lives, but I think I can be good for them." Then she added, "We've got to get married soon. I can't stand not to love completely, in every way."

# Wednesday Two Days to Game Time

I was worried and I have to admit it'd been a tough week. First there was Hunky King and his bad knee. I had to have Hunky. I couldn't stand the idea of not having one of my best athletes ready for the state championship game. When he came by my office without his crutches I danced around my oak desk. Hunky laughed at me, then held up his hand and said, "Wait a minute, Coach, it's not all that good, yet."

"Well, how is it, Hunk, 'you going to be ready Friday?"

"I sure hope so, Coach. The knee's still sore and I can't run on it yet, but it's improved a lot in the last two days. I think that cortisone is takin' away the inflammation that was there. The doc says he's not sure if it'll be ready."

I didn't need anything else to worry about while I was sweating out Hunky's knee, and then the physics teacher told me Matt Priest wouldn't be eligible to play unless he made up some work in physics lab. If he didn't get it all done successfully, he couldn't play on Friday. Matt hadn't completed some experiments he was supposed to have done, had been told repeatedly that they must be finished with good results, and that a passing grade depended on it. The physics teacher didn't like sports or athletes, but in this case he wasn't picking on Matt. The boy had just failed to do work he should have done, had been warned repeatedly, and deserved to be in hot water. I called Matt in for a talk.

"I've heard about your trouble in physics class from Mr. Reynard. Suppose you tell me about it."

"Aw, Coach, he's just pickin' on me. He don't like football players and he don't like me. He's just tryin' to screw up our game for Friday night." Matt shifted from one foot to the other, looking out the eye level window.

The tall athlete, so fast on the field, had earned a reputation for just getting by. "That's not the way he tells it, Matt. He says you've goofed off on several physics experiments and just haven't completed them. Is that true?"

"Well, yeah, in a way. I don't like physics. I wish I'd never taken it. He doesn't explain it in a way I can understand it, and the book is like readin' a foreign language."

"How much time are you spending on it at home, son?"

"I don't really work on it at home, Coach. I try to do all my school work in class so I won't have to take any books home."

"Boy, you can't pass any subject as involved as physics if you don't study at home. You've got to read every page at least three times. I know when I took physics, I would work every problem in the chapter and follow the book's examples on how to work the problems. You'll sure have a hard time figuring those things out for yourself. I guarantee you, if you don't spend at least four hours on every chapter, you won't know what in the world the author's talking about. If you only study here at school, you deserve to fail."

"I still think he's pickin' on me, Coach."

"Sit down a minute, Matt." At my request, the boy folded himself around one of the brown metal chairs.

"Son, I have to tell you the same thing Bruce Tucker told Streets a few days ago. Do you know how hard it is for a man to get a good job in the United States today? They're laying off hundreds of thousands of people from all size companies, and shipping the factories overseas or down into Mexico. People with master's degrees are walking the streets, looking for jobs that don't exist. A person has to choose some profession for which there's a demand, then become so good at it that he's better than almost everybody else, so he'll be needed for his expertise. These next few years are the most important years of your life because they'll determine whether you'll make enough money to scrape by or enough to live comfortably. Look around you in this town. You can see people who live from one paycheck to another, desperately trying to pay bills, stuck with a new car and payments, a new baby and hospital bills, a rental house where they're not building any equity, and a job that may be gone next week. How does that sound to you?"

"You don't make it sound too good, Coach. I guess I haven't thought much about it. I see people driving around in their new cars and living in nice houses. I figure only the dumbbells can't make a go of it."

"Matt, do you know who was the valedictorian of the graduating class at West Point last year?"

"Naw, Coach, I wouldn't have any idea, and what' that got to do with me?"

"It was a Korean immigrant girl, Matt. The anglos, people like you and me, we've often seen our parents and other people like us get by without a lot of knowledge or skill, and we think it's going to be that way for us. It's not, Matt. The federal government has forced us into an international economy where you'll be competing for jobs with all the people in the world, probably getting the same level of pay as the peon in Mexico or the laborer in China, unless you're extremely skilled in some area. The reason I mentioned the Korean girl is that the immigrants, especially the Asians, work terribly hard at their school work and they're the ones who'll be driving those big cars and living in those big houses. They're already becoming the doctors and the lawyers and the merchant chiefs, and if you keep on doing what you're doing, you'll be their yard man."

"Aw, you're kiddin', Coach." Matt laughed nervously and passed his hand across the sparse whiskers on his chin.

"Matt, I'm as serious as a heart attack. You'd better take another look at those physics experiments, finish them this week, and you'd better change your study habits and your attitude or you won't amount to anything. I've always liked you. You're a fine athlete and have a good chance to go to college on a scholarship, but you need to change. If you keep the attitude you have, you'll be just what I said, a peon in America. Get on up there and talk to Mr. Reynard and see how quickly you can get those experiments done." The boy left my office sadder and I hoped wiser.

At practice that day we didn't do any head-knocking because I couldn't tolerate any injuries. First and second-string offense ran plays for precision and the defense worked on the four defensive formations we liked to run. We used a five man front with two formations; both looked alike to the other team but we used very different tactics with our outside men, our nose men, and our linebackers.

We also practiced what we called our victory defense that we used when we were ahead and the other team was passing desperately.

I thought we looked mediocre in practice. The spark just wasn't there and I couldn't tell what was missing. I didn't really want the team to be terribly excited, just confident. Maybe the confidence was what was missing because all the team had read the newspapers and knew that Inland was favored. I had to remind myself how good we were to keep things in perspective. I knew Inland couldn't match our team speed even though they had Black and White in their backfield, and they were both state class sprinters. They didn't have Hunky King, but then we weren't sure we did either, and I wouldn't trade Horst Michler for any two players they had. I felt that our coaching staff was superior to theirs, even including myself. With his speed, passing ability and experience, Buck Callahan had to be the best quarterback in the state. When I thought of all these advantages, I sure wasn't pessimistic.

It was chilly and I didn't want the team to stand around too long in the cool wind. I had them get down on one knee and told them this: I want you boys to take a good hot shower, dry your hair good and get home as quickly as you can, because we sure don't need any flu or colds. Eat sensibly and get plenty of sleep. Don't have any dates before the game because you don't need anything to take your mind off the ball game." The team laughed when I said that, because they could understand the deeper meaning of my words without drawing them a picture. A hundred yards away, I could see through the chain link fence to the palms standing on the edge of the lake, blowing in the wind. Speedy Johns and I had chosen well when we came to Citrus City, it had been everything we had hoped it would be.

# THURSDAY ONE DAY TO GAME TIME

THE SUN HAD NOT POKED ITS PUNISHING HEAD over the horizon when Streets awoke. He lay still, enjoying the cool air coming through the partly opened jalousie window near his bed. He loved the cool air, the feeling of cold water splashed on his face, the briskness of a cold morning in the groves. He lifted his powerful arms out of the covers, moving them in the delight of knowing how strong he was. He looked through the window at the dappled moonlight on the Japanese plum tree outside his window and it gave him pleasure. God had been good to him in so many ways, and he was just beginning to realize it. The room was still dark except for a rectangular shaft of light from the moon, showing the outlines of a chair on the far side of the room. His brothers were still sleeping the sleep of youth, needing nothing but their good health to give them their needed rest. He thought of his brother Jonathan, developing some of the same muscular build and speed which had given Streets his notoriety. Jonathan was slightly thinner but was going to be taller than his older brother. Man, was he going to make a fine high hurdler. Streets was proud that as he began to study at home, his brothers and sisters were following his lead, more often bringing their books home, becoming more interested in their lessons and their grades.

He heard his mother in the other room, stirring around in the kitchen, starting the coffee pot and boiling eggs for their breakfast. God had been good there too. His mother had been so terribly hurt and was almost back to full speed, working at the sectionizing plant as she had done for many years.

The sounds coming from the kitchen were comforting to Streets. The clinking of the silverware on the dishes, the audible bubbling of the coffeepot, the accompanying aroma of the coffee, like that which drifted through a billion homes every morning. Gertrude Jackson was singing as she prepared the children's breakfast, her rich alto voice filling the home with notes that brought tears to Streets' eyes. He'd never thought of it much before, but she sure could sing pretty. "Amazing grace, how sweet the sound, that saved a wretch like me." Streets smiled at the idea that his mother was a wretch, whatever that was.

He went to each of his brothers and shook them gently. They didn't want to get up but that was part of being a growing boy. He saw to it that each was on his feet, had them make the beds, then went into the bathroom to shave. He had to be in and out of the bathroom in a hurry because it was a busy place at the Jackson house before school. The girls took twice as much time in that hub of activity as the boys, and there was always some contention about who was next. "Mama, Rosalie won't git out of the bathroom." Streets was a big help to his mother, the kids didn't talk back to him when he told them what to do.

When they sat down to the big breakfast of eggs, grits, ham, biscuits, and some reheated beans, things grew quiet. They ate well. There was no car, no telephone, and very few dress clothes, but they always ate well. Streets looked around at his family and realized he loved them. The idea never occurred to him before. He had always been protective of them, but in a proprietary manner.

He thought of tomorrow night's football game wondering how Hunky was doing, whether he would have his dynamic friend on defense with him at kickoff time.

Across the neighborhood, Hunky lay in his bed as the sun peeked over the horizon. He moved the sheet aside and lifted his leg, bending at the hip and at the knee. There was very little pain. He flexed it a few times, putting his fingers behind the knee, pushing on the ligaments and the tendons that were attached. He moved his foot to the right and to the left, testing it for pain. He got out of bed, put weight on the foot, then paced back and forth. He couldn't deny it, there was still some pain, but at least he could walk somewhat normally. Maybe if they taped the knee real good, it would see him though the ball game. He half squatted, then raised his body, did two partial knee bends, then flexed the knee again. He could do it even though it hurt a little, but he couldn't tell if it would stand up under game conditions. He didn't know how to play halfheartedly, had always gone at sports full bore. If he was able to play, watch out Daytona Inland. They'd wish they'd never seen Hunky King.

Coach Johnson awoke when it was still dark. The first thing on his mind was tomorrow's ball game. Even though God was always first in his life, controlling his attitude toward family, friends, school, athletes, his congregation, no one in his position could possibly forget the playoff game. Football had put him through college, had allowed him to move to this bustling citrus town, and had given him another way to reach people. Coaching helped him to be more effective as a minister. He hoped it never changed his interest from what was important to things which were unimportant. He didn't feel that God cared who won tomorrow night's ball game, and he had to keep it in perspective.

Caleb had paid a thousand dollars for his oversized bed. It took up eight feet of the eleven foot room, leaving just enough space at the foot to walk comfortably past. He rolled over, put his arm around his wife and drew her to him. She sleepily murmured and continued to doze. He kissed her on the cheek, rolled back to his side of the bed and put his size sixteen feet on the floor. He stretched, touched the ceiling, and thought of chinning himself on the doorframe, then thought better of it. He had pulled one board off the wall that way.

He pondered who he would put in the ball game in place of Hunky King, if the Hunk couldn't play. He had two or three choices, but none of them could fill King's shoes. And what about Streets? Would he come up to the level of play he had shown in the first half of the season? He could be counted on for defense, but would he play like he was possessed as he had in the Ocean City game? He was very happy that the Jackson family was attending his church. Gertrude Jackson seemed a good woman but she almost had more than she could handle with eight children and it was no wonder she had neglected going to church before. Caleb wondered what he would do if he had eight children. Thinking about it, he said out loud, "Hoooeeee."

From the bedroom came Sandra's voice. "Did you say something to me?"

Caleb laughed and answered, "Yeah, I said how'd you like to have eight children?"

Sandra, still looking sleepy, immediately appeared in the kitchen doorway. "What in the world are you talkin' about?"

"I was just thinkin' about Gertrude Jackson and her eight children. How'd you like to have that responsibility?"

"Ohh, that's better. What made you think of that?"

"Well, I was just thinkin' about Streets and all of the emotions he's experienced lately, and I thought about how glad I am that the Jacksons are coming to church, because they certainly need to include God in their lives, and they need the stability it can give them. Then I got to thinkin' about Gertrude Jackson and her problems, so that's the sound you heard. That lady's got a lot on her plate."

At five foot ten and one hundred seventy pounds, Sandra was a good match for Caleb. She had been homecoming queen her senior year at Grambling, a beautiful, peace-filled, helpmate to Preacher Johnson. She walked over to where Caleb was filling the teapot, put her arms around him and said, "If you get a chance to adopt eight children today, how about giving me a call so I can think it over for a few minutes?" They both laughed but they knew there was some seriousness in what they were saying because they had considered going to work in an orphanage.

Caleb didn't have a better friend in Citrus City than Bruce Tucker. Bruce had talked to him the day before about his approaching marriage to Natalie Shires and Caleb was glad. Bruce had been lonesome and sad looking and it was about time he had another woman in his life. He said as much to Sandra. "You know Bruce Tucker's going to get married, don't you?"

Sandra was properly surprised. "Nooo, I didn't know that." She smiled and said, "How wonderful. Natalie seems like a really nice person and Bruce's kids need someone nice. Those two appear to be very compatible, but you told me earlier that her mother was opposed to the marriage. Has she changed her mind?"

"Not so's you could tell it." With this, Caleb gave a mirthless laugh. "She's makin' life miserable for Natalie, tryin' to get her to say she won't marry Bruce. She's even threatened to move back to Toledo, but Natalie's stood her ground. Says she's going to marry Bruce if her mother moves to Moscow. It must be hard on her to be so happy about the marriage and so unhappy that her mother keeps actin' like Natalie's doing somethin' really bad."

At Lake Honey Mobile Home Park, Natalie and her mother were preparing breakfast, each one getting her own, maintaining a tension filled silence. Amanda would sob occasionally. When she did, it was both loud and pitiful. Finally, Natalie put her toast in the trash and the milk back in the refrigerator, poured her coffee in the sink, and walked back to her bedroom. After she gathered her gradebook and the papers she had been grading, she walked out the front door without any communication with her mother.

I knew there were many things going on among the people at school. If I had known all the details, I might have been more confused than I was. I sat in my little office, my mind in a turmoil, my belly churning. Tomorrow night's big game controlled my life. I thought of all that had happened to Streets lately. His mother's accident and near death, his run in with me and his turning his back on the team; these were critical events in his life. The run in with the English teacher could be good for him because he learned that you make people happier if you're nice to them than if you're mean or rude to them. Maybe in the long run it had all been good for him, but he had really put us through the wringer. A cool breeze came through the ground level windows, and I could hear the welcome sound of a mockingbird coming from a bush nearby.

I was glad when Hunky, Streets and Jonathan trooped into my office because Hunky was walking stronger than the day before, and I was glad to see Jonathan with Streets. The younger brother was already developing into an excellent athlete; maybe the two would be good for each other.

"Hey, fellahs," I said. "How's it goin' this morning? And Hunk, how's that leg?"

They laughed at me, knowing I was nervous. Hunky answered for them. "My knee feels stronger today, Coach. I did some modified sit ups when I got up this morning and it only hurt a little."

I told him, "We can see how it does at practice today. If you can't run on it today, there's not much chance you can play on it tomorrow."

"I'm sure you're right, Coach, but I think I can run on it."

"How about you, Streets, 'you ready to go?"

Streets stood with his arms folded across his chest. When I saw him I thought of Tarzan and Superman with their bulging muscles, but I never told him that. Up to now his head had been so big he didn't need anyone telling him how great he was. Still, I could sense some difference in him, and it seemed for the better.

"Yes, sir, I'm ready, Coach. The whole team is. Just think about it, Coach Warren; when you came here five years ago, did you figure you'd be playin' for the state championship?'

"Well, I sure hoped we would. You know Coach Johns and I were together at a small school in Tennessee where we had a limited number of athletes, so when we had the chance to come here, we jumped at it because of the good facilities and the excellent number of athletes available to us. We're lucky to have so many mature seniors and have such a smart coaching staff, and we've been really fortunate not to have many injuries this year. It's all come together to put us in the championship game. I'm glad to see y'all but you'd better get on to class. We don't want to make those teachers mad at anybody." The boys laughed at me but they hurried off toward their classrooms.

I had a friend in Daytona Beach at Seaview High School. He had coached football there for many years and knew what kind of a team Inland had. I called him to see what he thought of Inland.

"I've got to be honest with you, Angus. It's the best balanced football team in this part of the state. It's no wonder they went through the season undefeated, because they're good at everything. We all laugh at Black and White because of their situation, but there's nothing funny about the way those two scat backs can run the ball. You can't defend against one of them because if you do, the other one will sting you on the next play. They laugh at the teams that do it, running one of those yard eating plays, then slapping each other on the back, getting a real bang out of it. I don't know if their quarterback's as good as yours, because Callahan's known to be awful good, but their guy's a powerful passer and a good runner, so he'll try to keep you off balance. Their field goal kicker has kicked eight this year, the longest over forty yards, so they can hurt you that way, too. Honest, Coach, I wouldn't know where you could take advantage of any weakness."

I told the Seaview coach thanks for the information and went up to my class on creative writing.

At practice that afternoon, I had the coaches go over the scouting report on Inland. We ran against a team we'd set up to duplicate their running and passing plays, then worked on how we were going to try to block their punts. I went over the rules on the kickoff so we wouldn't make any dumb mistakes. Coach Johnson talked about clipping and reviewed blocking assignments to be sure they knew them perfectly. We surely didn't want one of our players going for a long touchdown, only to have it called back for clipping.

I had Hunky run around the field a few times and run in his position as we practiced. He limped a little and I could tell it hurt but he never complained and I knew if he couldn't stand to work out on it some today, he'd never be ready for the game. I didn't plan to use him full-time if I didn't have to.

# Friday Game Day It's Now or Never

**20** TO 7 IN FAVOR OF DAYTONA INLAND AND I had already seen enough of Black and White to last the whole season. It wasn't that we had played badly; this was one tough football team. The game was one quarter and two minutes old and Inland had the football again.

We had scored on our first possession, driving the ball right down the middle, mostly on the back of the Franklin Powell. Callahan had thrown a couple of short passes in the drive, and they had spread out just enough to let Powell carry us to the touchdown. Streets had run the ball three times, gaining three or four yards at a time, but had not broken loose for one of his spectacular runs we needed so much.

After our opening TD, Inland had gone to work like a machine. They were doing it mostly on sweeps, using a modified wing T formation, and from it the two well-publicized backs showed us how they had made their reputation. I had Streets playing the outside linebacker on one side and he was stopping them after short gains, but since I was holding Hunky King out part of the time to rest his leg, they were able to run the other end, away from Streets. I once switched Streets from left side to right to compensate for their success in that direction, and they just ran away from his linebacker spot. They were well coached, there was no doubting that.

Their quarterback was a lanky kid named Marsh. Black lined up at his left halfback spot, took a pitchout from Marsh, then swivelhipped his way around right end for eight yards, down to our forty-one. These two running backs were like fireplugs, neither one was over five eight and about as easy to tackle as a greased pig. The middle of our line had shut them down pretty good, so we were forcing them to go outside, and even if they were successful at that, maybe we could wear them down.

We were playing in Daytona where so many of the state playoff games had been played. It was just a two hour drive from Citrus City and we had been able to sleep at home, not having to go through the change in routine that often upsets a team. The crowd was strictly partisan and a big portion of the fourteen thousand who watched the game was cheering for Inland. Maybe I should say screaming for Inland, because the din was deafening. The night was ideal, cool but not cold, a great night for football.

Marsh hollered out his signals above the noise of the crowd and took the ball from the center. He made a fake to his right, then passed to his left to the zone where Streets was playing. I think they must have begun to take Streets for granted and nobody dared do that. He intercepted the pass and ran it up the sideline into the end zone without an Inland player laying a hand on him. Streets usually made a big display for the fans after a touchdown, letting them know who had scored. This time he knelt for an instant, then ran back to the huddle. Matt Priest kicked the extra point, making the score 20 to 14 still in Inland's favor, but causing us to breathe a little easier.

If Streets' touchdown made us think the tide had turned in our favor, we had better think again. Inland started in right where they had left off, running Black to the right and White to the left. If we did something to counteract their offense, they immediately changed their strategy and it kept both our team and our coaches off balance. From their thirty-five, Black ran the ball to the forty, and White came back in the other direction, advancing to the forty-eight. Then Marsh threw a sideline pass, this time away from Streets who had stung them once, and their fleet split end ran the ball to our forty-three. They tried to go over Michler's tackle spot and made nothing out of that. Black took the pitchout and ran the right end again, this time for fifteen yards, down to our twenty-eight. White gained four to the twenty-four, then Marsh passed over the center for six more, putting the ball on our eighteen.

We dug in and held them for three downs and they brought in the field goal kicker the Seaview coach had told me about. He was a Cuban, a soccer player recruited to be a field goal kicker and he sent the ball screaming through the uprights from the twenty-six, making the score 23 to 14. The Inland band blared their fight song and the fans screamed their approval.

On the kickoff to us after the field goal, they purposely kicked away from Streets. It was a short kick and Johnny Blocker took it at the thirty, advancing it to the thirty-eight.

I had Callahan start mixing his passes and he did a superlative job. He started with a look-in pass over the center to Terry Foote which was good for six yards. Then he came back with a sideline pass to Matt Priest for seven more and a first down at their forty-nine. Our side of the grandstands had been noisy as usual when the game first started and during our first touchdown drive, but they had quieted when Inland started moving the ball so well. Now they began to shout their approval as we drove toward the Inland goal. I asked Coach Speedy Johns what he thought we should do.

"You've got Franklin at the halfback spot, Angus. If I were you, I'd pull him out and stick Streets in again, and pass to him. Callahan's doing a good job and they're protecting him well, let's see if we can't get Streets into the end zone."

It sounded good to me, so I pulled Franklin out and put Streets in and I could hear screams of approval from our fans. Inland was really moving with our quarterback, so I ran the twenty-four counter at them and Blocker took it to their forty-four. Buck ran Blocker again, off the other tackle and they stopped him for a one yard loss, back to the forty-five. On third and six I had Buck run the screen pass. He ran it like it's diagrammed in the play book, letting the charging linemen almost get to him when he flipped it to Streets. An electricity filled the air as the fastest running back in the state gathered in the short pass just past the line of scrimmage, cutting to the right to avoid a defender, then moving back to his left, displaying both his power and speed. The defensive halfback hit Streets at the thirty yard line but bounced off as if he had run into a concrete post. Streets wouldn't be denied. He crossed the goal line with both hands high over his head, holding the football in one, then pumping his arms in exultation. He raised the ball over his head as if to spear it into the ground, then dropped it gently on the turf. The Citrus City fans roared their approval, and the band was the loudest I had heard them all year. For a change, the Inland fans were the ones who were quiet and I was thankful for that.

We needed every point we could get so I decided to go for two. I sent Franklin Powell to try to ram it in but there was a mixup on the exchange and we fumbled the opportunity away, leaving the score Inland 23, Citrus City 20. With that score it would take a touchdown instead of a field goal to win the ball game.

With a minute and twenty seconds left in the first half, we kicked off to Inland, and White brought the ball back to midfield on the kickoff, wringing a groan from the Citrus City fans. They used the sideline pass to perfection and ran their two speedy backs enough to confuse us. As the horn sounded to end the half, White crossed the goal line and we dropped further behind. Their extra-point try was good and the score was 30 to 20 in favor of Inland. Make that two touchdowns to win the ball game.

At halftime, I didn't have any spellbinding speech to inspire the team so I asked Caleb to talk to them. The big man's words were, "You fellahs are playing a good ball game and we're proud of you. I know we're as good as they are, we just haven't proved it yet. Remember, they've got to be afraid of what we can do to them, because we've scored three times on them and they can never let up. I want King to go full time on defense, maybe we can shut down that Black and White business. If Hunky's leg cramps up on him again, I want Michler to take the outside linebacker position on his side. You're doing a great job and we're proud of you. The state championship is what you've worked for since you were in the eighth grade, and it's now or never." The big man paced back and forth while the room stayed quiet.

"Let's be tougher and smarter. Play clean but play the toughest you've ever played. Let's not make any mistakes. Remember, it may be mistakes that make the difference in the ball game, so if there are any mistakes, let Inland make 'em. Now, let's go out there and win a ball game!"

We kicked off to Inland to start the second half, then held them at the forty and they had to punt. Streets took the punt on our thirty, running it back to our forty-three. I could feel electricity in the air as both grandstands became quiet, aware of Jackson's potential to break the big one. I left Streets in at the tailback spot and he began to give us a lesson in what you do with a football. He had regained the tremendous energy that had been lacking since he walked off the team and since his mother's accident. Callahan pitched to him running right and he went around right end like a race car circling the track over at the speedway nearby. He slashed for twenty-five yards on that play, then took a pass over center for another eleven yards, putting the ball on the Inland twenty-one. Callahan ran Blocker off tackle for three yards and two men hit Streets sure that he would have the ball. They could assign two men to Jackson if they wanted to but it made little difference. On the next play he ran the ball straight up the middle, deep into the end zone. Then he ran the extra point and we had closed to within two points, 30 to 28. From our stands, programs and hats flew through the air as the jubilant fans showed their excitement.

There were eight minutes left in the third quarter when Matt Priest kicked off to the deep left man, White. He went only three yards before Hunky King creamed him at his own twenty-one. Black ran the ball toward his right end where he had been so successful, only to be met by Streets, a yard behind the line of scrimmage. White ran left end, having no success as Hunky ground him into the turf after a gain of two. They tried the center of the line and Michler sent their fullback to the sidelines with a bruised thigh. They lined up to punt and we set up with a scheme we had used before to block it. I put Streets in the inside linebacker spot on the right and when the center sent the ball back to the kicker, Streets charged their defensive left guard as hard as he could, knocking him back about four yards to his left. Hunky King went barreling through the hole where the guard had been, racing at the kicker full speed. At the same time the ball met the kicker's foot, Hunky barreled into him, knocking both the ball and the punter backward. Parelli covered the ball on Inland's eight yard line and our fans went wild.

Callahan sent Blocker over right guard and he went to the four yard line. On the next play, Streets took a direct handoff from Callahan, faking it into the line, pulling their defensive backs toward the fake, then racing around right end, crossing the goal line without anyone touching him. Now he was the Streets of old, a powerful, shifty, slashing running back.

Priest kicked the extra point, making the score 35 to 30 and our fans were ecstatic. They were seeing Jackson return to the intensity he had shown last year and in the early part of this season. Our band played number after number and the Inland band answered in an effort to help their team change the tempo of the ball game, as it looked like it was flowing our way.

There were two minutes left in the third quarter and Inland wasn't dead. On the kickoff, with excellent blocking, White brought the ball back to their forty. On the first play from scrimmage, they faked a reverse and Black took a sideline pass, running it nineteen yards to our forty-one. Coming back in the other direction, they threw to White near the left sideline and that was good for eight more, down to our thirty-three. We had seen Black and White run the ends and take passes near the sideline so much that we forgot about the inside and you can't do that. Our defense knew that the first-string fullback was out with that bum leg, so I guess they thought the second-string fullback was just for show. On the next play he showed us something, running the ball down to our eight. That got our attention and it took them seven plays to put the ball in the end zone, turning the score around again, because after they kicked the point it was 37 to 35 as the third quarter ended. Maybe the momentum hadn't changed.

I sent in word to try to fake the sideline kickoff return, using Streets as a decoy, with Matt Priest carrying the ball in the other direction. Matt was one of our players who could run the hundred meters under eleven seconds, so if they thought Streets was the only dangerous runner we used on kickoffs, they'd have to adjust their thinking.

They were gun shy where Streets was concerned and you couldn't blame them, so when they kicked off and saw our wall form down the right sideline, they zeroed in on Streets like ants going to syrup. Matt took the ball from the right hand deep position, starting to his left as Streets started to his right as if to take the handoff from Matt. If I could have put myself in the mind of one of those defenders trying to stop the play, I'd probably have headed for Streets, and that's what they did. They almost ignored Matt and he took the ball down the left sideline to their forty-seven before being tackled by the player who had kicked off. Streets was gang-tackled and I was afraid he might be injured, but he jumped up from the pile like a kangaroo, laughing at their mistake.

We ran the screen pass with Streets taking the ball at the line of scrimmage, weaving and twisting his way from the forty-seven to the thirty-four, shedding tacklers left and right. He ran with fury, not a fury born of anger but I could tell his fury this time was delight. He knew he was powerful and fast and was enjoying the knowledge of it. On the next play he finished the job, taking the ball off tackle, bouncing a lineman away, then cutting left in front of their deep right defender, crossing the goal line again, knowing he was in familiar territory. After the kick we were ahead again, 42 to 35.

There were nine and a half minutes left in the ball game. I'd never have thought they could score thirty-five points on us because we were too good on defense. I'd have sworn we couldn't roll up forty-two points on them either because from our scouting reports, and watching their game films, they were also too good to give up that many points. Still, it had happened and that 42 to 35 score was no fantasy; it was a fact of life.

The crowd didn't know what to think when we kicked off to Inland. Both teams could score and it looked like whoever had the ball last would win the game. They took the ball up the field into our territory with violence that would have done justice to a television detective story, driving the ball to our twelve before our linebackers gave the crowd a lesson in defense. Wary of any gambling play outside, they ran the ball off their guards and tackles using those two marvelous running backs. When they had moved it to our one, with four plays to put it across the goal line, they ran a quarterback sneak. Hunky King put them back on the three with a bone jarring tackle that sent the quarterback to the sidelines to try to get well in a hurry.

It was still second down with just three yards to the promised land and they must have felt some confidence. Their right end ran deep into the end zone, then came back toward the playing field and the quarterback zipped the ball at him like a bullet, a pass that almost couldn't be knocked away. Still, Streets managed to get a hand in front of it and it bounced away harmlessly. Third and three. Black ran straight at the line and tried to catapult over it, only to be met by Michler at the two, and they got no brass ring on that play. That set up fourth down with still two yards to go, and they must have felt like gods of football were against them because they had run seven plays inside the twelve with still no touchdown. When they ran White over the guard from the left side, even though he jumped as high as I'd ever seen a back trying to reach the goal line, Streets met him with all the power contained in his Atlas-like body, grinding him into the pile of players, well short of the double stripe.

Holding them solved one problem for us; we were still ahead in the ball game with five minutes left. However, we had ninety-eight dangerous yards to go to score again, and we knew we mustn't do anything that would give the ball back to them. I put big Franklin Powell in at the fullback spot with instructions to hit them with all the power he had, and he did. He went off right tackle on a slant play for eight yards, then ran off left guard, good for four and a first down at the fourteen with four minutes, thirty-two seconds left. Streets then solved our field position problem in the best way possible, running the ball eighty-six yards in the most brilliant single play I had seen in all my football career.

He would not be denied. He must have been hit at least ten times, covering more than the eighty-six yards as he twisted and turned, reversing his field so often that it would be hard to recount the play. All the two and four hundred meter interval runs he had done at track practice, all the gene-blessed physical ability came out in the run. I knew there were many college scouts in the stands and they must have drooled at the sight of this most blue chip of blue chip athletes showing them what he could do. He was a fine baseball and basketball player, and would be recruited for these sports, too, but I knew his heart was in football. Teams from all over the country would be worrying him and his mother for weeks when the time permitted to recruit came around.

With the score 49 to 35, and with four minutes left, we kicked off to Inland. Our defense was inspired by the goal line stand we had just displayed, and Inland couldn't move the ball past their own twenty-eight. With three and a half minutes left on the clock, they had to kick to us and their punter must have been asleep because he kicked the ball to Streets who gathered the ball in at our thirty-nine and ran it in for another touchdown. We missed the extra point but the score was 55 to 35, the most comfortable margin we had all night. I pulled Streets out of the game and the Citrus City crowd went wild. One of the finest displays of sportsmanship I'd ever seen happened when not only our fans, but the Inland spectators gave him the biggest ovation I'd ever seen for a high school athlete.

That's the way the game ended, 55 to 35. All our dreams had been realized, and I felt we deserved it. Caleb Johnson and Speedy Johns had worked so hard, and they were good for the players they coached. I had put in my years, learning how to handle athletes properly, demanding good physical training, a thorough knowledge of the positions they played, and demanding the best grades possible from them. There was no better way and we knew it. I still didn't think God cared who won a football game and I could never pray for victory, but he had answered my prayers in a lot of ways.

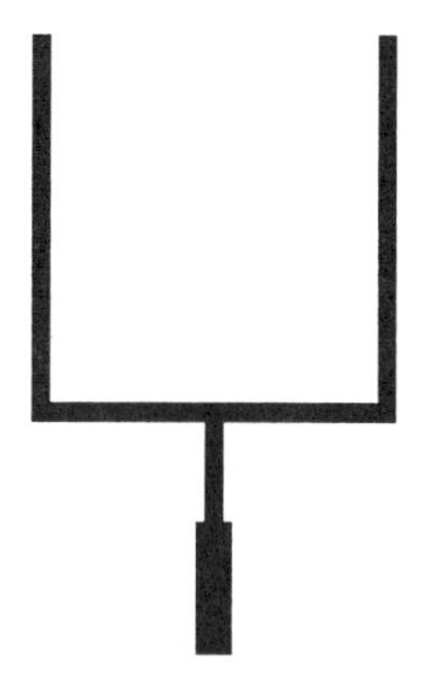

# EPILOGUE

WHAT A THRILL! WHAT A RELIEF! WHAT ultimate satisfaction flooded each of us coaches and each team member. We had worked daily for years to reach this pinnacle in high school football, and we had arrived. In Florida with its burgeoning population, where a thousand people move in every day from other places, and where hundreds of new schools have been established, our school had won the prize they all wanted. We were the 5A football champions.

Every day of practice, every weightlifting session, each wind sprint, each coach's scouting trip on some long road that lasted past midnight, had led to this moment and our happiness was palpable.

We had hung together through every routine practice session, through every learning experience as the players had changed from boys to young men. Their bodies had developed from straight and lean or chubby, to muscled and powerful, and their understanding of the game of football was as good as we coaches could instill in them.

When the day came that the recruiters were allowed to sign high school players, eleven of our gridders were picked up by the colleges. Streets, Michler, Hunky King, and Buck Callahan were recruited by teams all over the country, and all signed with big schools. Streets and Hunky signed with Florida State, Callahan with the University of Florida, Horst Michler with Penn State and Foote, Franklin Powell, and Priest with the University of Miami. Four of our players were quickly picked up by smaller schools that had good football programs.

We who had coached the team received some offers, too. Caleb Johnson had many calls to become a line coach at major universities but felt that he was serving people the best he could where he was. Speedy could have gone as head track coach to three colleges that he told me about, and I could have rejoined my old school in Tennessee, but we decided we were happier, though certainly poorer, at Citrus City High School. We coached other champions in both football and track. We often discussed how blessed we were and tried to understand why God would pick us out in the special way He had, but we never figured that out.

Bruce Tucker and Natalie eloped the night of the championship game, though they waited until it was over. I really think Natalie would just as soon have read about the game in the paper instead of attending, but they stayed until the electrifying end. They went to the Florida Keys to snorkel and skin dive on the reefs close to shore. I don't think that's all they did because Natalie came back with a glow that hasn't left her yet, and I received the impression that a good time was had by all.

Natalie's mother was never satisfied with Bruce. He was always too skinny, too old, too any excuse she could muster, and she had permanently lost her whipping girl. I observed that the old lady became a lot easier to get along with when Natalie had two babies of her own and Amanda became a doting grandmother.

Then there was Streets Jackson. He came to understand himself much better as he was guided by Caleb Johnson. The meanness left him, but not the fire. He learned that an athlete can be a dynamo on the playing field and on the track without being a dirty player or a terrible-tempered Mister Bang. He quit popping people on the chin, though he did have days when some of the bad temper would well up, then he'd realize what he was doing and could laugh at himself. It wasn't easy, but it happened.

He went on to star at FSU, both on the football field and at the track. He became a world-class sprinter and qualified to compete in the Olympics. He signed with Green Bay in the National Football League and quickly learned what cold weather really is. With his signing bonus, he bought his mother a luxurious new house and changed the living standard of his family so much that when they compared the old with the new, they couldn't believe their good fortune. He purchased Gertrude a new Cadillac, and though Jonathan begged Streets to buy him a car, he would not. He told Jonathan that a student with a car usually paid more attention to the car than to his books, and he wanted Jonathan to be an honor student, which he was.

Jonathan became six foot six, supple, and fast. When Streets left for college, Jonathan became the one who insisted that his sisters and brothers be good students, and he hounded them so that they were. He set a new state record in the high hurdles and followed Streets to FSU.

Gertrude never changed her friends. May Ann still dug at her and they had many laughs together. Gertrude liked to drive her Cadillac to the Good Will store because that's where the bargains were. She shopped the nice stores, too, but she still liked the Good Will store. Streets bought the red-roofed board and batten house next to the railroad tracks and gave it to his mother for a rental house. When he was in Citrus City, he liked to visit the old house and get the feel of the days which were often so bitter to him.

Streets never became a showboat. He liked being an example to children and wouldn't refuse a public appearance if he thought it would help someone. Whenever he saw a young athlete who had a chip on his shoulder, he would often take him or her aside and relate how his life had been affected by his early attitude and his transformation. He helped a lot of people.

Strangely enough, Latisha and Streets both went to Florida State. As Streets' understanding of life and his personality changed, he became acceptable to Northella Washington. Latisha became a math teacher and a bit of a celebrity as her students called her Mrs. Streets Jackson.

As for me, the whole experience of winning that first state championship was enormously moving. When I thought of Streets and his personal torment and of the agony he had put us through, I cried again as I had the night he walked off from the team. I awoke as Blackie shook me and I realized I was in the lounge chair on the shore of my lake. She had leaned down to hold me in her arms and ask me what was the matter. I still sobbed a little as I told her nothing was the matter, but that memories were almost more than I could bear.